OPEN DOOR

OPEN DOOR

Iosi Havilio

Translated by Beth Fowler

Afterword by Oscar Guardiola-Rivera

LONDON · NEW YORK

First published in English in 2011 by And Other Stories
This edition published in 2013 by And Other Stories
www.andotherstories.org
London – New York

Originally published as *Opendoor*
© Iosi Havilio, 2006

English language translation © Beth Fowler, 2011
Afterword © Oscar Guardiola-Rivera, 2011

The rights of Iosi Havilio and of Beth Fowler to be identified
respectively as Author and Translator of this work have been
asserted by them in accordance with the Copyrights, Designs
and Patents Act of 1988.

ISBN 9781908276032
eBook ISBN 9781908276070

A catalogue record for this book is available from the British Library.

Supported by the National Lottery through Arts Council England

Supported using public funding by
ARTS COUNCIL
ENGLAND
LOTTERY FUNDED

CONTENTS

ONE

When the owner of the veterinary surgery told me to go to Open Door to examine a horse, I didn't argue with her. The idea appealed to me. Open Door. It sounded strange.

I left Plaza Italia at around nine in the morning, with a sun as hot as midday overhead. First I took a long-distance coach, nearly an hour and a half of slow progress with a thousand interruptions, as far as the bus station at Pilar. It was full of people, the air conditioning was broken and there was a strong smell of ammonia. Someone showed me where to catch the local bus, which didn't leave for a good half hour. On the road again, open country to the right, open country to the left, a roundabout, then another forty minutes until we reach Open Door. Outside the bus window, the plains, the gated communities and the cattle pass by.

The bus left as I crossed the railway lines. It was ten to twelve. A girl with plaits and chubby cheeks was watching me wide-eyed. As if she were there to welcome me. She was standing by the window of a house-cum-kiosk, under a green and white striped awning, half her body in the shade, the other half in the sun. She watched me as she chewed her gum with concentration, lips pursed.

I smiled at her but she didn't react. She hardly blinked. I averted my gaze, looking in no particular direction: an unpaved street, straight and long, which eventually lost itself in the distance, where it was starting to cloud over. It was going to rain: sooner or later, it was going to rain. On the other side of the tracks, I was surprised by three giant silos, which looked as though they had been dropped there by a fleeing helicopter, three concrete monstrosities, apparently useless, but still standing. To my right was an area of intense green undulating woodland, threaded with zigzagging paths, like snakes. A few blocks away, a man on a bike appeared from a side street, his head covered by a pith helmet. As he turned, he raised a cloud of dust which followed him for a few metres and then faded away.

Could it be here? I have no idea. I turn round and the girl stops scratching at the earth with the points of her sandals, which reveal her tiny, overlapping toes.

Is this the way into town? I say out loud. The girl doesn't answer and I don't know whether to continue. Perhaps she's deaf, I don't know. I persist: Excuse me . . . Yes, this is it, she concedes unwillingly. She speaks with her back to me, seeming to watch me with the nape of her neck. She enters the house and reappears ten seconds later inside the window, stretching her thin arms across its full width, between the frame and the display of sweets.

Do you need a taxi? she asks. No, I say. The silence lasts as long as I can endure, but inevitably I start talking again: I'm being picked up. And her: Oh, good, she says and continues watching me, her eyes wider than ever.

There was another silence and I asked again, just to annoy her: Does the train pass by? Every now and then, but it doesn't stop, just keeps going, she replied and immediately pursed her lips again and set about chewing her gum, determined not to utter another word.

The conversation ended there and although I made my way off along the edge of the road, for a long time I could feel the soft breeze of her gaze behind my ears. Those eyes bothered me.

It was already midday. The heat was becoming too much. And a light summer headache gripped me, ran through me, coming and going, from temple to temple. Just in time, I heard a rasping hum, somewhere nearby, but out of sight, as if someone had cleared their throat to begin talking. Like a purr.

Jaime is going to turn onto the street bordering the railway tracks in his truck or *rastrojero*, his pick-up, he's going to stop in front of the house-kiosk, he's going to get out, he's going to look at me, dejectedly, and he's going to wave hello.

We recognised each other immediately, it wasn't difficult. I'm late, he says, or apologises, I don't know which. It's five past twelve, I say and, judging from the look in his eyes, with their mud-spattered lids, he doesn't know whether I'm reproaching him.

As soon as Jaime starts the engine, the girl with plaits appears at the window of the house. I can see her in the rear-view mirror.

Jaime grasps the gear stick and yanks it roughly in all directions, to free it I suppose. His hand is thick, with the rough skin of a reptile. He steps on the accelerator and the engine groans, gives a start and then dies. Jaime clenches his fist and hits the steering wheel gently, puffing through his pitted nose. He manhandles the truck once more and, after another false start, it stops protesting and begins to move.

This is the main street, Jaime explains to me, raising his voice to drown out the barks of the two or three dogs that are struggling to catch our wheels as we drive the first few metres. This is the shopping centre, it closes at half twelve, then no one opens up again until after siesta, half four. Here's the school.

We covered what must have been the ten or fifteen blocks that made up the main street and, where the tarmac veered off, Jaime took a dirt road, the natural continuation of the previous one. Some five hundred metres ahead we turned right onto a narrow, single-track road, perpendicular to the one we had been following, guarded on one side by an endless line of almost uniform wire fencing, and on the other by a row of very tall poplars concealing a polo field flanked by low stands. Jaime stopped the truck in front of a gate and, without getting out, explained the confines of his land.

Straight ahead, behind the stable, there's an olive plantation and on this side there are a few ranches, most of them abandoned. Further along this road there's a shop, opposite there's the polo field, and behind, where the fence ends, is the lake. Jaime got out to open the gate and paused for a minute looking towards the lake, the latch in his hand.

On the way to the stable, Jaime tells me that the horse is called Jaime, like him. He blushes a bit as he says it. He falls silent, regretting having mentioned it. He opens the stable door, but doesn't go in, pointing out the horse from a distance, saying that he'll wait for me here. I tell him he doesn't have to, that he can come with me if he wants. Jaime fixes his eyes on his packet of tobacco and concentrates on rolling a fat cigarette. I don't insist. I'll go and examine him, I say, and Jaime responds with a long drag. He waits at the entrance, one foot inside, one out.

The other Jaime is a Creole-Spanish cross, aged between eighteen and twenty, a fairly common horse, with no distinguishing features. I listen to his heartbeat, the rhythm is normal. His pupils are stained a pale yellow and there's the start of a burst blood vessel at the bottom of his left eye. He looks anaemic. But there's something else, something conclusive. He watches wearily, docile, with the same expression that the other Jaime must be wearing behind me. I examine the tail to confirm a hunch: nodules between two and three centimetres in diameter spread along its length. I tell Jaime, who comes closer, I ask if he wants to touch. They're melanomas, I say. He doesn't ask anything, either he knows or he doesn't want to. I go on: It's a tumour that affects the tail and it's common in Spanish horses. A tumour, repeats Jaime. As long as it doesn't spread or reach any vital organ it can be treated, I explain. Jaime says nothing, he's moved round to the other side of the horse and is stroking its back. He doesn't look at me. I continue: There is medication that can delay the process, corticoids. But it's irreversible, replies Jaime. I don't know whether he's asking or telling me. Yes, sooner or later, I say, but not immediately. There are cases where the tumour dissolves with no explanation. One in a thousand, I add so as not to give him false hope. The light is very dim and the horse's mane appears darker than it must be in reality. The reddish tone of the head distinguishes it from the rest of the body. We'll need to do a scan to give a more precise diagnosis, I say and Jaime raises his gaze with mild, almost imperceptible annoyance, as if I'd been hiding something from him. Equine scans are very expensive and I don't feel it's worth it, I think to myself without saying anything. Jaime's eyes melt into those of the animal, becoming straw-coloured and sickly.

It's one forty-five. The bus driver told me that instead of returning to Pilar I'd be better taking a local bus to Luján, and from there catching the train or the Luján coach service.

Are you hungry? asks Jaime and comes back round the horse. We go outside and the harsh sunlight hurts our eyes, just like the blinding light in cinema foyers when the film ends. In the sky, a tiny light aircraft crosses the horizon and leaves a soapy trail that fades at the tip. A white foam, whiter than the clouds. It's like being somewhere else.

He used to race *cuadreras*, says Jaime as he cuts salami into thin slices, gesturing towards the stable with his chin. Now I can see him up close: the flat face, clean-shaven, and the very hairy neck and chest. Jaime must be married, he must have a wife and two or three children, but there's no sign of them.

An oblong window covers a good part of the kitchen wall and looks out onto open country. My eyes close. I resist for a while, until I begin to doze. I come and go, between sleep and the green world on the other side of the window. Jaime stays quiet, he doesn't intervene. I can feel his presence nearby but it's as if he weren't there.

At some point a dull thud rouses us and forces us to pick up the conversation. He talks, I listen.

Jaime tells me that he has a scythe and, now that he doesn't have a fixed job anymore, he's devoting his time to weeding the plant nursery at the colony. I have no idea how many years it's been abandoned, it's practically a forest, he says. I wonder what the colony could be but Jaime changes the subject:

'It's carnival next week. We still celebrate it here,' he says, and I smile.

It's gone five and I don't understand how it got so late. Jaime takes me to the Luján bus station in his truck. So that you're not too late, he says. Where the dirt track meets the road Jaime turns left and a few metres on, he slows down. There's the entrance, the nursery is over there at the back, he says, pointing out a large iron arch with a sign in the middle: *Dr Domingo Cabred's Psychiatric Hospital Colony.* It's like a village within a village, says Jaime with a half-smile on his lips, the first I've seen him give.

We pass the rest of the journey in silence, the lights of nightfall staining the windscreen. Before saying goodbye,

I ask Jaime why he didn't call a local vet. He shrugs and climbs back into the truck, which purrs away again as it did at midday.

From a public telephone in the bus station, I call Aída's number. I didn't have a good day, I'm low, she says from the other end. She wants to talk, to chat. I tell her that I want to go to the cinema like we said. She hesitates, I insist. We arrange to meet at quarter to eight in the bar on the corner of Avenida Córdoba and Montevideo, half a block from her house.

The return journey seems quick, drifting in and out of a sleep that mingles with flashing images of the motorway: a shopping centre that looks like a mock spaceship, a service station just like the shopping centre, various toll barriers so similar that I get confused, and a silver-coloured tower that flashes past too quickly for me to work out what it is.

Aída is waiting at the door of the bar. She sees me arriving, I'm about fifty metres away, diagonally across the street. Aída looks the other way and lights a cigarette, pretending not to notice.

'You have to be honest with me . . .' she begins to say, but she's interrupted by the waiter. We order a beer. Aída is about to speak again, but I cut her off with the first thing that comes to mind. I tell her the hamster story, a true story. Aída lights a fresh cigarette, looking like she has something to say, but she resigns herself, swallows two aspirins, and listens to me.

It was a few weeks ago, at the end of December, a Saturday morning, and the owner of the surgery had gone away for the weekend, between Christmas and New Year. It was almost one o'clock and since I was alone, I closed up a bit early. I'm dealing with the till, the cash, the receipts and all that, when I hear someone shaking the door handle trying to get in, I play dumb and hide behind the counter, so that they don't see me. I'm not about to open up. I count to thirty. They've gone, that's it, I get back to what I'm doing. But soon I hear a knock at the door. Hard, desperate knocking. I go to answer it, I have no choice. On the other side of the grille, there's an old woman with a tiny face staring at me. I tell her that we're already closed. I don't care, she says rather hoarsely. I want to see the owner, she says. I tell her that the owner isn't here, to come back another day. That won't do, it has to be now, she says and it's as if her voice is giving out. From her small, old-lady's handbag, she produces a package wrapped in newspaper. She opens it slightly, just enough for me to catch a glimpse of hamster, stiff, rather crushed, on its back. I'm revolted, by the animal, by the old woman, and most of all by that little package, and I tell her that it would be best for her to come back on Monday and speak to the owner. But it's too late, the old woman gets mad. Some kind of spasm takes hold of her, her eyes cloud over, her veins swell up, she looks like she's about to explode. And she shouts: The lousy thing didn't even last a day. I try to calm her, but that makes it worse. Drop dead, cheap bitch, she says to me and sticks her hand through the grille, dangling the hamster in the air.

Iosi Havilio

Aída bursts out laughing, coughing a bit between drags. We compose ourselves and look at each other again. She says: See, we have a laugh together, don't we? And I nod, to humour her.

Afterwards we went to the cinema and saw a really bad film.

We ate in a Creole fast food restaurant of the most decadent kind and got drunk on the worst wine possible. We slept together, naked and embracing.

The next day, Aída disappeared.

TWO

In the dark, Aída looked a certain way. In the daylight that look changed and she became sad again. The light exaggerated the angles of her face and her natural pallor. In the half-darkness, as she was when I met her, surrounded by other bodies, Aída struck me as an attractive woman, tall, sinuous, with bony shoulders and a wide forehead. When I saw her up close, as she spoke to me, I began to focus on her details: the tip of the sharp nose, the slightly uneven teeth, the broken, desperate eyes. Aída almost didn't have skin it was so fine, like silk paper, laying bare her veins.

We met by chance in a bar on Calle Reconquista on the first day of the year. I had gone in without planning to, partly because of the rain and partly because I'd been wandering for quite a while and was starting to get bored. I ordered a glass of wine and settled myself at a corner of the bar, right in front of the till. In a while, a foreigner with a heavyset face and freckly nose sat down next to me and offered to buy me a couple of drinks. He was twenty-something and smiled a lot, too much. He wasn't bad, but definitely not my type. In a moment, he said in that kind of bad Spanish that some foreigners speak: '*Acá, todavía es mejor.*' I laughed, of course, and he stared me in the eye, almost serious. I'm going to the toilet, he said in English and didn't return.

The rain had stopped and I'd decided to move on when Aída appeared, elbowing me so hard that I spilt what was left of my wine down my blouse. I also took a little bite out of the glass. A strange sensation, rather unpleasant. Aída whipped round quickly, appalled, slightly drunk, and I think she spilt some of her drink on my trousers too. From that moment on, Aída didn't stop talking. How awful, was the first thing she said. She grabbed my hand and led me to the toilets, barging her way though the crowd. She took a cotton bud from her handbag, wet it with alcohol, and brushed it several times across my lower lip, which was only bleeding slightly. It's nothing, just a tiny cut, she was saying. She offered me a cigarette and we smoked in front of the mirror. Me, sitting on the edge of the toilet with my legs swinging; her, leaning against the wall. She asked me everything at once and I replied to some of her questions.

Aída tells me that she doesn't know why she comes to these parties, that they're always the same in the end, people crushed up against each other, barely able to move. I didn't know, I say, that it was a party. When we left the toilets, Aída brushed her fingers over my lips again. She didn't need to. Come on, let me buy a round and we'll forget the whole silly incident. The silly drink, she corrects herself and laughs.

Aída repeats three times that she's a photographer and works freelance for a couple of fashion and decorating magazines.

'What about you?'

'I was going to be a vet, but now I just work for one,' I say and she immediately takes an interest. She tells me that she has a twelve-year-old dog called Diki whose paw had to be amputated last November because it got caught in the spokes of a bike.

'I'm going to catch a taxi, can I take you anywhere?' Aída asks after a pause. I tell her no, thanks anyway, I still don't know where I'm going. She insists.

'Why don't you come for a drink at my place while you decide?'

I let her lead me. The rain, which has come back with renewed enthusiasm, convinces me.

Aída's place was a two-room affair in Calle Montevideo, half a block from Avenida Córdoba. An old building with a very tall door of black iron, two or three stairs covered with a red carpet and a traditional lift with a rectangular mirror at the back.

When she opened the flat door, Diki jumped up at her, pawing at her legs. Aída bent down to cuddle him and Diki responded by licking her cheeks. I had seen many dogs in my time, but never one like this, ugly as well as lame.

'Do you like anisette?' Aída asked. 'I love it,' she answered herself and filled two small glasses decorated with gold crescent moons. Two Turkish glasses. Anisette seemed like an old-fashioned drink to me, and now that I could see her clearly, under lamplight, it felt appropriate: Aída had something old-fashioned about her too.

She raised her glass, I raised mine and we clinked them. I don't quite know how Aída ended up massaging my neck, and my back, her hands like pincers. She did it very well, like a professional. She poured me another glass, and, as she unbuttoned my blouse, she asked:

'You don't mind, do you?'

We spent a long time on the sofa, listening to music, talking nonsense, initially without touching each other, then later, on her initiative, playfully intertwining our legs. Aída's were long and slim. Another glass of anisette and Aída leant her head against my shoulder. She asked me to stroke her. To the touch, Aída's skin confirmed something that had caught my attention when she was near me in the lift. Her cheeks were covered in little transparent flakes, like puff pastry. Aída suggested we lie down on her bed. We'll be comfier there, she said.

Clothes always lie. Or rather, if they don't lie, at the very least they conceal. Aída undressed. And if she had seemed a fairly normal girl before, well formed but normal, when I saw her naked, straight on, I was surprised by how small her tits were, like toys, as if they were only there because anatomy demanded it. She sat down on the bed and started rolling a joint. Get in if you want, she told me, and when I saw her from behind, I found her tiny knickers hilarious.

Then she embraced me and I let myself be embraced. She wanted to kiss me on the mouth. Not today, I stopped her, maybe another day. She didn't protest. And all that time, as we smoked in silence, until I fell asleep, I couldn't stop thinking about Aída's skin, which changed every other minute, which she shed like a serpent.

That same week, without giving it too much thought, I moved into her flat.

THREE

On Sunday we woke up at half two in the afternoon. Why don't we go out for a bit of air, said Aída from the bedroom, her voice still not clear from last night's cigarettes. I was sitting on the toilet, flicking through one of those women's magazines that published Aída's photos. By some miracle, I didn't have a hangover.

OK, I said, let's go. Aída came into the bathroom, looking wide awake. I'll make coffee, she said, stroked my forehead and left. I stayed in the bathroom for some time, engrossed in an article about a new equestrian style in women's fashion which had been all the rage in Europe for years and which, according to the journalist, was going to land here at any moment. One photo, filling a quarter of a page, showed a blonde model, practically albino, her hair pulled tightly back like a ballerina, posing with her mare. I immediately thought of the moribund horse in Open Door and his owner, the two Jaimes, whom I had met the day before. I imagined them together, lying on the straw, keeping each other company right now, while Aída was making me breakfast.

I took the magazine into the kitchen to show Aída. Look, I say to her and she makes a contemptuous gesture with her hand. It was a joke, to piss her off, she didn't like horses, even in photos. As a girl she'd had dreams, dreams of horses that she'd never tell me about. She called them dreams, but they must have been nightmares. I persisted anyway: I didn't tell you about the horse from yesterday, I said, the one I went to examine. Poor animal, I think it's got cancer. Aída pulled a disgusted face. And you know what? I said between sips of coffee, it has the same name as its owner: both of them are called Jaime. Aída laughed, thinking it was a joke.

Afterwards, while Aída showered, I had a second cup of coffee, black, no sugar, to wake me up a bit more.

Shortly before seven, I saw her for the last time. She was wearing faded jeans and a black T-shirt, she'd put her hair up in a kind of bun. She seemed happy, normal. Her breath was bitter, from an empty stomach.

We had gone to La Boca. We were bored, the walk had been a failure. Too many people around, too many noises all at once and nothing much to do.

At some point Aída went into a bar. She gestured with her hand, she barely moved her lips, she seemed to say I'll be right back, or something like it. I lit a cigarette. With my back to the street, I caught my reflection in a long and narrow mirror with traditional painted designs around the edge.

People passed to and fro and I disappeared and reappeared between them.

A blond boy stopped in front of me. He had a cigarette hanging from his mouth. He smiled at me and mimed lighting it with an imaginary lighter. I gave him mine. He couldn't have been skinnier, or dirtier. He was that type of blond whose hair is the only blond thing about him. A tough street kid, tanned skin, full lips, theatrical stare, aged about fourteen or fifteen. He lit his cigarette with the tip of mine and lingered longer than necessary in handing it back. He had a scar snaking between the knuckles of one hand. He didn't take his eyes off me. He looked at me the way some brats do, unintentional and yet intense.

'Fancy a smoke?' he said bringing his face closer, all his teeth on show. I just looked at him, a bit lost.

Do you want to or not, the boy pressed me and, because it was Sunday, because I was bored and because Aída still hadn't come out, I hunched my shoulders as if to say: Why not? The boy jerked his head for me to follow him.

First I glanced into the bar and amongst the crowd I saw Aída going into the toilets. What had she been doing all this time? It didn't surprise me, Aída did that sort of thing, disappeared, played hide and seek. The blond boy was waiting for me at the corner.

We took a diagonal lane and came to a yard that doubled as a basketball court, a few parked cars around the edges. The blond boy guided me to an out-of-sight corner where there were two other boys, even rougher looking and much younger. One was rather chubby with the look of an obedient dog, his face camouflaged in the hood of the tracksuit he was wearing. The third boy was much taller than the other two, wearing denim from head to toe, a proper show-off. Did you get it? the blond boy asked the one in denim, who immediately took a long, fat joint out of his pocket, twice the size of a normal joint. The blond boy lit up, took two deep drags and passed it to me. We smoked, each taking our turn, in perfect harmony. They asked me my name and I asked theirs. They told me that they lived round here and that they played in a band. They wanted to know where I was from. From far away, I replied.

Drugs don't always act the same way, it all depends on the person and the circumstances. The lad in denim, who had struck me as the most laid-back of the three, was retreating into himself. The fat one, on the other hand, had taken down his hood and was getting more and more excitable by the minute. The blond boy, like a good leader, didn't seem to be affected.

'We want you to suck us off,' the little fatty said out of nowhere, projecting the not-yet-fully-formed voice of an overweight adolescent.

The blond boy released a smoke-filled laugh. The one in denim turned pale, then red. All the blood rushed to the fat boy's head, enough for the three of them. And he laughed too, through clenched teeth. As I didn't say anything, didn't even move, their nerves finally got the better of them and they passed me the joint again. The round continued without comment. When the joint had finished, we said goodbye with a kiss on the cheek, like good friends.

FOUR

It was getting dark. After my adventure in the yard, I went back to look for Aída at the door of the bar. I went in, checked the toilets, looked around the tables, but nothing, not a single clue as to where she might have gone. I crossed the street and sat down on a bench on the riverside. I lit a fresh cigarette and, with the smoke inside me, the effects of the joint revived. I felt good.

I noted the time on my watch, five to nine, and started walking along the river. Up ahead, at the foot of the old bridge, not quite in focus yet, I make out a small crowd of people and a series of intermittent lights, now illuminating, now concealing them. I draw closer to find out what's going on.

The police have set up a cordon to contain the fifteen or twenty onlookers pressed up against the railings at the riverbank. Most of them are probably there because they've seen other people stop first. In the street, next to a patrol car, there's a fire engine and an ambulance with the doors wide open and a stretcher spilling halfway out onto the asphalt. All the lights are flashing: those on the patrol car very quick and blue, the fire brigade's lazy and red; the lights on the ambulance aren't revolving but flash intermittently, green and white. Together they merge, ricocheting off the opaque water, colouring the iron skeleton, creating sparks on the rust. The sirens are silent.

Like the others, elbow to elbow, squeezed into the narrow gully between bodies, I too lean against the railings. Like the others, I look upwards. Not just anywhere, but at the top of the bridge. I can't see a thing. What's going on, I ask. I can imagine what it is, but I'd prefer to be told. The lady next to me gestures with a finger and says: Up there, in the middle. I still can't make out anything, the night is closing in, thick and starless. What's going on, I ask. And the woman, whose face I now see is full of wrinkles, a red scarf patterned with arabesques knotted round her neck: There, walking on the ledge, can't you see? Her voice is cracked, scratchy. There, look, he's moving, on this side. Yes, I see, I'm starting to see. Nothing more than a shape, thin, with a point on top, slightly less black than the rest. That must be the head, then what I can only assume to be the torso, the arms, the legs, now I'm just seeing what I want to see. Because in truth, it's exactly the same as before, just a shape moving slowly, clumsily, like an old machine with a broken engine.

In a minute, someone else appears next to the old woman, who has stopped talking now – a lad of around twenty in a blue sleeveless t-shirt and shorts with a pattern similar

21

to that of the woman's scarf. He's wearing flip-flops and both his hands are busy, the one closest to me with a pizza in a box, still sealed, the other grasping the hand of a little girl in a yellow bikini, who, although she doesn't look it, must be starting to feel cold. Does he want to jump? asks the lad, without looking at me. It looks like he wants to jump, he answers his own question. And then immediately, to the little girl: Don't look. And the girl: Why, I want to see. The old woman starts talking again, without taking her eyes off the action up above: Look, and she points again, a bit higher up, as if she wants to reach the bridge with her hand. He's moved across from the other side. Right in the middle, see? To think that he's so young, says a new voice, a bit further over, a woman, not so hoarse as the one here next to me, and much fatter, a fake pearl necklace holding in her double chin. How can it be? she asks herself, or us. Nobody responds apart from the little girl: I see her, daddy. Is it a girl, daddy? I don't know, and don't look, I told you. How old is she daddy? And the father, who seems too young to be a father, is trying very hard to see what his daughter distinguished so quickly. Look, daddy, there's another one, on this side. Is it another girl, daddy? It's true: another shape appears on the stairs on this side of the river, then another, and another with a flashlight. These forms are much bulkier than the one in the middle of the bridge. The old women can't see them, they're getting desperate, and in this observatory, thirty or forty metres away, a contest begins to see who can guess the next move. There are cries of: Look, there are three of them, they're surrounding him. There's one further down, the other two have climbed higher up. Look, look everyone. And everyone has their own story. From behind, a tall man in a mechanic's uniform of worn blue confirms in a fluty voice that the person wanting to jump is a man, that his wife is in the ambulance having a panic attack, and even ventures: He must be desperate. Do you know him? The woman with the fake pearl necklace doesn't contradict him, she takes his word for it and follows the action. A fireman without a helmet seems to be directing the three rescuers' mission from the base of the bridge through a walkie-talkie. At his side, a man from the coastguard, his light brown suit clinging to his body like a glove, issues instructions to his men who are floating in a small boat, quite precariously, circling aimlessly without lights under the arch of the bridge. Here and there they dodge clumps of water hyacinth. In order to communicate, the man from the coastguard forms a megaphone with his hands. We can't make out a word. Further over, beyond the red and white tape, which blocks the path with the word danger every ten centimetres, there's another group of people, smaller than ours, but among which can be discerned an old woman, a not-so-old woman, a mature man, another younger man, and two children rather than one. They don't, however, have our secondary group of curious onlookers, who don't dare approach the railings, preferring to remain protected by the darkness, but who comment, murmur and speculate all the same. Like the cars and buses, which, before turning into the avenue some fifty metres ahead, slow down without actually stopping, resembling a funeral cortège. Some drivers are in too much of a hurry and don't have time to pay attention to the patrol cars, or the bridge, or the police cordon, far less to what is going on up above, and give three sharp blasts on their horns, as they would in celebration, to hurry on those ahead.

For a while nothing changes on the bridge. Some people get impatient, the girl wants to go, she's hungry. And the father tries to lighten the mood with a joke at which no one laughs: Come on, mate, make your mind up, my pizza's getting cold, he says to the person up there, who, of course, doesn't hear him. Or maybe he does, because not a minute later we begin to notice movement once again on the crossbeam of the bridge. Two of the firemen stay at the highest point, illuminating the scene: what can they see, what are they planning, I wonder. The third is just a few metres away from the person threatening to jump, and he begins a game of push and pull, coming and going, in which one advances and the other retreats. They know, like two fencers contemplating one last, fatal lunge, that to touch the other would be to finish everything. The first must be saying something like: Stay there, I'm not going to do anything, I just want to talk to you. And the other: Come any closer and I'll jump. Each wants the other to stay where he is. But until when? It's a blind impasse, with no solution. One knows what he wants, the other, seemingly, does not.

It's half nine and once more the action builds to a viscous nothing. I don't want to think any more. I don't want to and yet I wonder whether I should do something, try something, approach the fireman speaking into his walkie-talkie and ask him something. But what?

The lad with the pizza announces: He's not going to jump at all, you'll see. And he takes the girl's hand again, turns around and departs, not without glancing back once or twice as he walks away; surely it can't happen right now, not after waiting so long. But no, he's right, it doesn't look like anyone's jumping after all.

In a while, the man leading the operation on the bridge takes the initiative again. The suicide case isn't putting up as much resistance as before. He's getting tired. The fireman advances a few steps and must be speaking to him. I wonder if he has something prepared or whether he's improvising a few words on the spot to say that everything can be worked out, nothing's final, except for death. No, not that, the word death can't be prudent in such circumstances, better to avoid it. And the jumper will say to him: No, nothing has any meaning. A difficult argument to refute.

Now a small spark appears between the two. Look, explains the old woman, he's lighting a cigarette and passing it to him. See? Yes, a tiny ember that weakens and revives as the smoke is drawn in or exhaled illuminates the black point that is not quite yet a head but which shows up against the black of the bridge and the blue-black of the sky. The shape smokes and breathes. Anyone would smoke at a time like this.

I put my hands in my trouser pockets to fish for my cigarettes, and with one in my mouth, we're equal, from a distance. Two pairs of lungs filling with smoke. I feel calmer, he's not going to jump, it's for the best. The threat of a storm also seems to have passed right by.

I count: one, two, three long drags. Some, like the

woman with the fake pearl necklace, have resigned themselves to not seeing anything and move away slowly, along the edge of the cordon, noiselessly, with a certain respect. Somewhat frustrated, perhaps.

And the taste of the cigarette in my mouth, rough on my palate, reminds me that I haven't eaten anything since breakfast, that Aída and I meant to have lunch together but we couldn't decide, lunchtime passed, and I was still hungry, even more so after the joint.

The too-young father and his daughter in the yellow bikini must be munching their pizza in front of the television by now, while they tell the young mum about the time they wasted in vain at the foot of the bridge. And if I leave, I'll buy a pizza on the way and surprise Aída.

But just then, as I'm about to go, the old woman with the scarf grabs my arm, gesturing upwards with her nose. Look there, behind, the one next to the one with the flashlight, see? the woman says to me in a low voice, as if there's any way he could hear her. Yes, I see, one of those crouched down a few metres behind the jumper, positioned on a higher beam, either because he has taken the decision alone or because he has received a signal from the head of operations, moves, only just at first, then suddenly tries to catch the smoking figure with a swipe that doesn't quite reach, and everything that follows is too quick, too inconceivable. For the last time, the guy, or girl, hesitates. The glow of the cigarette can no longer be seen, he lets go with one hand, swings a leg over the rail and, just in time, before they can grab his other arm, he lets go and falls: he is falling.

Here, love, the old woman orders me as she covers her eyes with the scarf and pulls on my shoulder: Don't watch, love, you'll never forget it, ever. And yet I watch, I can't stop watching. And I follow the fall with my head, my legs that bend by themselves, and the rest of my body that crumples without letting go of the railings. And in four seconds, not too fast, not too sudden, he gives a single twist in the air, turns face down, spreads his arms and legs, and slams against the sheet of putrid water which, with the impact, seems more like metal than liquid. Like a toppling crane or falling bell tower whose echo rolls on and on, further and further away.

Between my eyes and the rippling black water, my left arm crosses my face, wanting to obscure my vision, but only showing me my watch: nine forty-five. Quarter to ten, not a minute more, not a minute less.

I'm almost sitting on the ground, I don't know how I ended up so low down. I straighten up. The other one doesn't surface. Instead, bubbles cluster around the hole into which he vanished, either because he's still breathing, or because the river has swallowed him and is now belching.

My gaze shoots upwards again, the three firemen are still in the same position as they were a minute ago. One shines the flashlight downwards. And for an instant, the rings of light seem to go crazy, darting all over the place, eventually getting lost in the overcast sky, as dark as the river.

Here below, more directionless than ever, the crew on the vessel, no longer receiving the encouragement of their superior, are attempting an impossible, labyrinthine, futile course. One of them holds a lifebelt of almost phosphorescent orange tied to the boat by a white rope, and, as a gesture, he throws it into the water. He doesn't know where or to whom.

On the other bank, a boatman, who has followed the action from the island half erased by the night, launches his dinghy to help in the rescue. To no avail, because the coastguards, protective of their official capacity, send him away with a gruff shout, to which the boatman responds with insults as he withdraws.

The old woman retied the scarf she had used to cover her eyes, and refastened a shoe that had somehow come off during the fall, and once more she grasps my arm: You'll see, dear, I told you, you'll never get that image out of your head. She lets go of me and departs, annoyed.

The boatman, still in the dinghy but closer to his bank, starts to gesture desperately towards our side. He shouts, he can't be heard. Too late, the helmetless fireman, who has already hung the walkie-talkie from his belt, takes heed and notices an enormous, flat prow advancing inexorably towards us. And despite the coastguard's cries, there is no way to stop the sand dredge with its circular cabin. Nobody noticed it, focused as we were on the fall, unable to see anything else. It's now making its way up the Riachuelo river, passing beneath the bridge, rocking the ridiculous little rescue vessel with its impotent, disbelieving crew and erasing with its sharp keel all trace of what the river has just swallowed. The captain of the sand dredge, unaware and blameless, sounds the siren three times. Just in case.

And when the echo of the final siren fades, as if there hasn't already been enough noise, the sky cracks, heavy with clouds. I shiver. The water hyacinths tremble and head off in search of open water, along with the small islands of rubbish, the plastic bottles, the tyres and everything that can be swept along by this muddy, carnivorous sluice. Within a few minutes, the calm of a moment ago becomes a furious, voiceless commotion, cold and glutinous, that rakes through us inside and out. The wind shakes the earth and its sediments, the smallest bits of detritus search out our eyes and above and around us we see nothing more than the confused memory, more or less horrific, of what just happened.

I leapt back onto the street and caught the first bus that passed, which, by chance, was going my way. There were no passengers, the driver was alone, listening to the radio at full blast. I sat at the front.

Intrigued by what he saw reflected in the rear-view mirror, that confusion of lights and shapes, shrinking into the distance, the guy asked me: Did something happen?

Someone wanted, I say, to throw himself off the bridge.

FIVE

From the smells, the creaks and the mechanical, laboured breaths multiplying around me, I knew it was the middle of the night. The middle of the night, in one of those strange pre-dawn hours, and I knew that if I wanted to I could open my eyes again. And right away I knew they had been closed for much longer than I could imagine. I could open my eyes if I wanted, but not yet, I resisted. I was returning from a deep and pleasant sleep, my body warm and my head spinning. Everything weighs more than usual, my eyelids, my jaw, my ears, especially my ears, they're throbbing too hard, echoing a painful humming that starts in my temples, a cross between a lullaby and altitude sickness. Then, before anything else, before my conscience begins to string together the things I'm starting to take in here and there, a phlegmy voice, partly distorted and forming flecks of saliva, asks my name.

He says I fainted on a bus on Sunday night. He's a young guy, not more than thirty, with two- or three-day-old

30

stubble, a touch of grey lightening the lank hair around his forehead. He's wearing a white coat but he doesn't look like a doctor. He asks me if I remember what happened. I tell him yes, perfectly, up until I fainted I remember everything. He asks if I want to tell him anything. Not now, I say, maybe later. He asks if I know what day it is. Monday? He shakes his head with an inexplicable hint of satisfaction. Today is Tuesday the thirteenth of February. Tuesday the thirteenth, he repeats. Anything else? the guy asks me, his slanting eyes narrowed, yet shining intensely because of his contact lenses. I raise myself up, look him in the eye and he holds my gaze for a few seconds, then gets annoyed. I want to know when I can go home. He says it's nothing to do with him, I'll have to wait until the duty head finishes his rounds and anyway, I should be taking things easy. That's fine. Right, I'm going, he says, hanging his stethoscope, which he had put in the pocket of his white coat, round his neck. Why wouldn't I take things easy?

I'm surrounded by another ten trolleys, most of them occupied. Bodies passing through, like me, waiting to be discharged. My eyes close and I sleep again for I don't know how many hours.

In full daylight, a nurse wakes me up to take my pulse. She says that the duty doctor won't pass by for about an hour. I ask if I can make a phone call.

The owner of the veterinary surgery is all worked up when she answers, she says this isn't the way things are done, that if I had some kind of problem she'd understand, but that

I have to let her know, that's what phones are for after all, that yesterday afternoon she missed an important meeting with those people who want to start a rabbit-breeding business, the Dutch folk who don't speak a word of Spanish, all because I left her hanging and didn't let her know, didn't I realise? It's four in the afternoon on Tuesday, she complains, sighs, and repeats herself in more or less the same words as before. My call time is running out. Before we're cut off, she remembers that I didn't call her to tell her how I got on with the horse in Open Door either. You just disappeared, she persists. There are ten seconds left and I don't have any more coins, if I want to speak it has to be now, right now, five, four, three, I manage to say: I don't know what happened, and the line goes dead. I was going to tell her that I was in hospital and that apparently I fainted on a bus on Sunday night. She wouldn't have believed me.

I hang up the phone and it gives me back more coins than I put in. That's hospitals for you. I slot them all back in and dial.

Aída's voice answers, recorded on the machine: *This is Aída, I'm not here right now, say what you want or call back later, bye.* I hesitate for a second but I don't leave a message. There's too much to explain.

They discharged me at six in the evening. Before I left, the duty doctor asked me if I took drugs.

As soon as I opened the flat door, Diki threw himself on top of me, making a superhuman effort to support himself on his single back paw. He was like a wild beast, or at least as wild as a disabled dog confined within four walls could be. It was a struggle to get him off me, but I managed to calm him down at last with some rice I found in the freezer. He was really hungry.

Everything was just the way we had left it on Sunday when we went out. In the kitchen, the dirty plates were piled in the sink and a bowl of peaches in syrup was now covered with a film of mould. The bedroom was the same as ever; the bathroom much dirtier, and the whole living room had become Diki's latrine. Either Aída hadn't been home or she'd abandoned herself to absolute neglect.

I sat on the sofa in front of the blank television screen, which reflected my whole body in scale. I looked a bit like an X-ray, ghostly, with no identity. I listened to the answerphone messages in an attempt to work things out. There were seven. The first two, blank: they hesitate then hang up. The third is from Beba, one of Aída's aunts who lives in Asunción, the only one of her relations I know of. She says: Aída, it's Beba, I arrived a few hours ago, you must be working, so, I'm going to walk around for a bit and I'll phone you later. I left my case at the bus station, so don't worry, I can get about easily. Can't wait to see you. Love, Beba. She spoke as if she were writing a letter, with full stops and commas. In the fourth message, I hear the voice of a man, who introduces himself with his full name, leaves his number and wants Aída to phone him tomorrow before twelve. He doesn't say why. The fifth is Beba again: Well, Aída, it's ten o'clock, you've not been in all day, you must have forgotten I was coming, never mind, we'll talk tomorrow, I'll see if I can get a cheap hotel in the centre. The sixth and seventh are blank: they breathe and hang up. One of them is mine.

I have a sleepless night, partly because I've already slept a lot and partly because I'm expecting Aída to arrive at any moment and surprise me. I feel like an intruder in a bed I've barely used. I try to empty my mind, I think about Jaime, the horse with the nodules on his tail, about the girl with plaits spying on me from behind the piles of sweets in the kiosk window. I think about anything to stop myself thinking. The bridge invades my thoughts, it's inevitable.

The phone wakes me at seven. It's Beba. I explain that I'm a friend of Aída and that I've been living in her flat for a while now. And Aída? I tell her that I haven't seen her since Sunday and that it doesn't look like she's been home since. That can't be right, I spoke to her on Friday and told her I was coming to visit. I don't know what to tell her. I'm coming over, she says and hangs up.

Beba's name suits her, despite her age. Her complexion remains so impossibly soft, so polished, like a newborn baby. Iridescent glasses, a silk scarf round her neck, magnificent nails, neat mouth, and yet so old.

It's just not possible, she says, nobody disappears overnight. We'll have to find her somehow. I have to go to work, I say. Beba tells me not to worry, that she'll take care of everything and we'll see each other tonight.

I arrive at the surgery at ten to nine, like a model employee. The owner is already there. She greets me with a grumpy look. I don't understand why she's so annoyed.

We need to talk seriously, she starts to say from the other side of the counter, but she breaks off when a guy, a bit of a punk, comes in carrying two enormous boxes that half cover his face. The owner gestures for me to take care of receiving the merchandise and locks herself in the bathroom. I sign the slip and the guy goes on his way. It's two packages of disposable syringes. The owner shoots out of the bathroom, even more furious than before.

'We have an understanding,' she says, 'a pact of trust.'

I listen without listening while I focus all my attention on checking the order. She doesn't tire of talking. The thing is that she gets on well with me and she doesn't want to fire me but I have to pull my socks up, because the foundation of work is mutual respect, so she told me.

'It's a two-way street, I place my trust in you and vice-versa.'

I don't know how many times she repeated the word trust. At one point she even became friendly, she came round the counter and seemed to be about to hug me. She scared me.

In a while she left. The rest of the morning passed without incident, the same routine as usual: an anti-rabies vaccination for an English Cocker Spaniel, two consultations on Siamese cats displayed in shop windows, a young salesman in suit and tie who left me free samples of a nutritionally balanced pet food that was due to come onto the market over the next few months, and a woman worried about her Great Dane's continual vomiting. White, lumpy vomit, she specified, excited by the rarity of the case. I told her to bring him in so we could examine him.

Without intending to, just to kill time, I started flicking through the appointments book and, partly by chance, partly because that's the way things happen, it fell open at J. The name Jaime jumped off the page at me. Just Jaime, no surname, and in parenthesis, 'opendoor', strung together, in lower case. I dialled once and there was no answer. I dialled again and heard Jaime's voice, which I recognised immediately despite the background noise.

'It's me, the girl from the vet's. I just wanted to know how the other Jaime was getting on,' I say and something tells me that this pleases Jaime at the other end of the line, he must like me speaking to him like this, in this familiar way.

'Just the same, lying down half the time.'

The silence that follows lasts for several seconds and is filled by ambient noise from both ends of the line: from here, the hum of the fan mingling with street noise, from there, the wind sweeping through the house.

The conversation is minimal, monosyllabic. The truth is that I don't know why I called, it's ridiculous, it's as though I'm flirting with him. But Jaime, when I've already said goodbye, see you, and I'm about to hang up, decides to say something else.

'Another examination wouldn't hurt,' he says and we agree that he'll call the surgery next week.

SIX

Aída's flat looks like new. The floors are shining, the kitchen spotless, as is the bathroom, the bedroom feels like a hotel suite, and even Diki gives the impression of being a relatively normal dog. By the looks of things, Aída has come home with renewed enthusiasm.

It's half eight, I make myself a cup of tea, change my clothes and flop down on the bed in the dark. Ten or fifteen minutes go by and sleep is beginning to overcome me when the doorbell rings so hard and suddenly that it makes me spasm as I imagine an epileptic would. I'm given no time to react before the bell rings again, this time supplemented by a couple of sharp knocks on the door.

It's Beba, she's upset and ignores me completely as she comes into the flat. She is escorted by two uniformed police-men, caps in hand. Beba sits on the sofa and lights a white filter-tip. She smokes using a cigarette holder. The policemen settle themselves on either side of the television, guarding it. They look at me, they look at one another, we all look at each other.

'Something terrible has happened,' says Beba, expelling smoke through her nose and mouth at the same time. She breaks off, making the most of the pause to take a drag, and continues:

'It could be that Aída's dead.'

The only thing that comes to me is to contradict her. It's not possible, I say and I become aware that I'm only wearing a blouse, no bra, very provocative. And immediately, or simultaneously, I realise that the two policemen realised this much earlier than me.

'I'll be right back,' I say out loud, to everyone and no one in particular.

I put on the first thing I find, tracksuit bottoms and one of Aída's jumpers with wooden buttons, and once more I'm back on centre stage with no time to analyse things first. One of the policemen, the less officer-like of the two, takes the floor.

'Apparently there's been a suicide,' he says in a bored tone, and the topic proves to be to be a familiar one. Beba waits for my reaction, rocking on the edge of the sofa, almost falling off it. The policeman proceeds with his report.

'Last Sunday an individual jumped off the old bridge in La Boca and, according to the firemen's statement, the description of the victim fits that of the missing young lady.'

Beba breaks down, bursting into tears. She stands up and I have to take a step backwards so that she doesn't collapse on top of me. But she reaches her arms out to me, she grabs me by the shoulders and lowers her head in search of consolation near my chest. Her nose is running. I don't know what to do, I don't know what to think. I prise Beba off me as best I can.

'It can't be true,' I say, 'I was there, I saw it all.'

In the police station we have to take a number. There are at least four people waiting ahead of us to make their statements. Beba managed to calm down on the way over here but doesn't utter a word to me at any point.

This part of the police station comprises a series of desks in a row and, behind them, an internal patio roofed by hanging ferns lit up with halogen lamps. Apart from one, which serves as a resting place for three piles of folders on the verge of toppling over, the desks are occupied by policemen concentrating hard on their official duties. Only one is using a computer, the rest make do with primitive typewriters in a military green. On one of the walls hangs a vast map of the city divided into different zones by thick, red lines. In a corner, in full view on a white, triangular shelf fixed to the wall, a plaster Virgin Mary with a neon halo watches over them.

Our turn comes and we're landed with a fat official. Beba takes it upon herself to explain the situation and the guy listens impassively, uninterested. Now I have to give my version of events. I don't know where to begin. I tell him about Sunday, that we went out at about four, that we went for a walk by the riverside, that at some point Aída went into a bar to pee and that I went for a wander. That afterwards, I went to look for her but never found her. The official types everything I say but he has to go back several times to make corrections because his fat fingers don't fit the keys and he presses two at a time.

Now that I look properly, I see that the plaster Virgin Mary is plugged in via a long cable that comes out of the back of her robes.

Beba nudges me, she wants me to talk about the bridge. I give a blow-by-blow account, as I experienced it, including all the details, up until I got on the bus. After that I fainted and slept for almost thirty hours in the care of the hospital, I say. They look like they don't believe me.

We are told that an as-yet-unidentified female threw herself into the river from the old bridge in La Boca at 9.45 p.m. on Sunday 11th February, that the duty magistrate has already intervened and due to adverse weather conditions the recovery of the body by the coastguard's divers has been postponed until further notice. What's clear is that, for the time being, Aída is still missing.

After walking several blocks in silence, we arrived at the door of the flat. By mutual agreement, Beba slept in the double bed in the room, and I took the sofa. Despite everything, I fell asleep straight away. That night I didn't dream.

The following day, too early, I was woken by Beba's legs, criss-crossed with a thousand tiny veins, sweeping back and forth in front of me behind a broom. It wasn't even seven in the morning. The television was on a channel showing the weather forecast. The storm wasn't going to pass until Saturday.

'I couldn't get a wink of sleep all night, this is all such a mess,' says Beba with a mug of coffee in her hand. I could barely look her in the eye, something about her was starting to repel me.

Beba kept talking for some time, it was her speciality. I finished my coffee without paying any attention, spent two minutes in the bathroom, dressed in the same clothes as yesterday and left for the surgery.

What exactly could have happened? I tried to reconstruct the events since Sunday on a piece of paper: the mix-up with Aída, the suicide on the bridge, the faint, the day and a half in hospital, my arrival at the flat, the appearance of Beba, the policemen. I went over the same thing a thousand times, trying to put my thoughts in order, to introduce some logic to the situation, but I didn't get anywhere. Was it possible that I had witnessed Aída committing suicide without realising it? Yes, it was possible, and at the same time both absurd and in bad taste. A hundred times I replayed the blurred yet indelible images of the negotiations between the firemen and that nameless body, which nobody could even confirm as male or female. I even found myself asking that jaded question, which sounds so stupid in other people's mouths: Why did she do it? Did she have a reason? Of course she did, everybody does. But as for proper reasons, what you'd think of as reasons, private, weighty motives, none occurred to me. She wasn't a happy girl, but that doesn't mean anything. Aída must be somewhere, playing hide and seek, sooner or later she'd appear, and all this delirium would become a dark and amusing anecdote. Things would sort themselves out.

At closing time, I repeated the usual routine: I switched off the surgery lights, lowered the blind, put the chain on the door, but I didn't leave. I didn't want to see Beba again, the very idea tortured me. I undressed and lay down on the consulting table. It was a bit narrower and a good ten centimetres shorter than me, but still quite comfortable. I fell asleep immediately.

I had a strange dream that lasted all night. A dream full of animals.

SEVEN

Saturday came round again and I went back to Open Door. This time I took the train to Luján. I phoned Jaime from the station. He took a while to answer. I was in the stable, he said and then told me that the other Jaime had been lying down all week but that he didn't look too bad. I'm in Luján, I told him. Jaime fell silent for a few seconds, then asked whether the café was open so I could wait for him there. I'll be out front, I said. I'll be with you in twenty minutes, he replied, with an enthusiasm that I'd never suspected he could summon, adding: It's a beautiful day. Jaime hung up and I couldn't prevent my mind from straying to that vivid image I'd had in my head all week of the two Jaimes frolicking in the sun, caressing each other's backs, snorting, each merging into the faded eyes of the other.

At the station's exit, I was approached by a bald man with heavy dark circles under his eyes, as if they'd been painted on with shoe polish. It was hard to tell whether he was a taxi driver or about to proposition me. Can I take you into the centre, he asked, confident that he would be taking me into the centre. Someone's picking me up, I answered, feeling protected by my reply. I crossed the avenue and felt a bit disorientated by the two-way street split in the middle by a small, elongated square, which broke off abruptly at the corners.

There was a nameless ice cream shop on the corner, makeshift, just opened for the summer. It had very few flavours on offer, most of them were empty and covered with paper. I asked for a cone of dark chocolate and lemon mousse. The chocolate wasn't bad but the lemon, too sticky to be mousse, had lumps of ice in it that bulked out the cone. I sat under a small tree which, when I leant back against the trunk, pushed back at me with hidden thorns. It was a *palo borracho*, a silk floss tree, and it was sharp. From here I could see a black iron bridge at the end of the station, connecting the two platforms, four or five metres above the tracks, useless for committing suicide. If Aída, or whoever it was, had chosen this one instead of the other, she would only have managed to break a leg, or both legs, or a hip.

On the way to the house, we stopped at the entrance to the loony bin, as Jaime calls it, to let them know that he wouldn't be tending to the nursery that afternoon. He told the guard at the gate, sticking his head through the window without getting out of the car. The man nodded from his little hut and we drove on.

The dirt track was still muddy from the recent rain and

the truck skidded from side to side, like a drunkard. Jaime was concentrating hard, gripping the wheel with both hands, his face practically pressed up against the windscreen. It was good fun.

We arrived at the gate and I moved to open it before Jaime did.

'I'll get it,' I said and he smiled. When I unhooked the latch from the post, I had a strange feeling, a kind of déjà vu.

Jaime made some maté tea and we exchanged a few words about the weather, the countryside and the city. Then we went to see the animal.

The other Jaime was lying down at the back of the house, in the open air. We approached slowly, respectfully. He looked weak, exhausted, and had deteriorated somewhat since last Saturday.

'I took him outside to see if the fresh air would do him any good,' I heard Jaime say behind me, in a resigned voice.

We led him carefully by the reins back into the stable.

'He's going to die tonight,' said the other Jaime. His eyes were shrunken, very red. I held out my hand to him and he didn't understand. And an impulse I can't explain made me embrace him. A little out-of-time, he reciprocated and for a while he patted my back with his big tanned mitts, as if he were stroking the horse's flank. I don't know who was consoling whom. My nose was pressed up against his neck and I could smell an unfamiliar odour, sour, stale and exciting. I grasped his arms and gently pushed him away a few centimetres: he was crying. I took his face between my hands and kissed him very close to his lips. Jaime closed his eyes.

I thought about how unusual the situation was, about those hands touching me, those arms squeezing me tightly, and about any number of other things. I thought that if I wanted to I could fall in love with Jaime. I thought about how he must be thinking about something too. About me? The horse? The burial? It will be a difficult burial, he'll have to do a lot of digging, he'll need help. Maybe the best thing is to have the horse put down and cremate him afterwards, keeping the ashes in a large urn. Wasting no time on agonies or ceremonies.

I moved away from him a little, I grabbed his hand, and with the other I gestured for him to follow me. I paused by a mound of straw a few metres away. Jaime stopped crying. I undid three or four buttons on my blouse. Jaime dried his tears with the cuff of his shirt, embarrassed and clumsy. His face changed suddenly, he almost laughed. I thought he was what you would call a decent guy. Jaime looked me in the eye, his lips trembled and he stretched out his arm without touching me.

'Let's go, it's getting cold,' he said and I didn't know what to do, feeling ridiculous with half a tit on show.

On the way back to the house, in a low, hoarse voice, Jaime spoke again:

'You'd be best spending the night here, it's very late for you to go back now.' He spoke the way gauchos must speak, no beating round the bush. I nodded, it seemed like a good idea, I was tired and had nowhere to go. I was in no danger with Jaime.

That evening, he heated up some stew, a bit dry, but tasty.

During the meal he asked me if I would mind sleeping in his bed with him. He said it would be more comfortable for both of us. The armchair, he explained, is too rickety. I smiled.

When we entered the bedroom, full of faded pictures and oversized furniture, the ceiling high above our heads, I sat on the edge of the bed waiting for Jaime to throw himself on top of me. He didn't. He touched me a bit, out of a sense of duty. That was it.

I wake in the middle of the night and discover a bronze crucifix hanging on the wall, which prompts a long shudder. How come I didn't see it before? I sit up in bed, Jaime is at my side, on his back, his teeth and gums on show. I have the urge to run my finger around his lips. And close his mouth. I'm thirsty. I don't dare to leave the room, this much silence scares me. I wrap myself tightly in the blanket which has fallen on the floor and I drop off again without too much trouble.

Morning brought a ferocious headache. Jaime heard me moaning, he tells me as he tips up the kettle and a torrent of steaming water cascades into the mouth of the maté gourd. It's a bright and shining morning.

'Were you dreaming?'

'Yes,' I say to reassure him.

Jaime passes me the maté. I feel good by his side. I ask after the other Jaime, whether he's already been to see him, he says yes, he seems a bit better, livelier, he even saw him eating enthusiastically. That made me happy and I even thought that perhaps the horse would survive a few days longer than expected.

'And you, did you dream?' I asked Jaime.

'No, not last night. But sometimes I do.'

'About what?'

'About anything, nothing really.'

'And what's it like?'

'Always the same.'

Jaime wasn't being honest, he was looking to one side, hiding something. Something in his 'nothing really'. Later, he left me alone in the house for an hour. I lolled in a canvas deckchair I found folded against the veranda wall. I stayed motionless the entire time, slack, forgetting about my body. The headache dissolved in the humid, mid-morning calm. Through the soft aura of the sunlight I could see the gate through which the truck had driven off, the row of poplars bordering the road, behind which a team of polo players was training, the sown fields, and farther away, in the distance, a long, low hovel, unfinished and badly made, with a corrugated iron roof and an electric-blue water tank connected by an orangey pipe to the back of the house, and infinite lamp posts, and all those wire fences before the horizon. The countryside, that was it: a jigsaw whose pieces could join together differently every time you blinked.

Jaime returned with a bundle of wood, a bag holding meat, lettuce, a pile of potatoes and sweet potatoes and some tomatoes. With him was a short man, with a flat face and almost no neck, the kind of guy who seems to have been formed in a mould. He took charge of preparing the barbecue, without speaking, or even looking much. A man whom Jaime called Boca.

'I have to go back this evening,' I said to Jaime after we'd eaten. He had his back to me, but I could sense his reproach. 'I have to work early tomorrow,' I explained, 'I'm expected at the surgery.'

Again he protested, silently, without getting angry. With one hand, his left, he grabbed a bottle of wine by the neck and filled a glass in front of his chest, which he offered to me with the other hand, without turning round. I waited. I wanted him to look me in the eye. How many seconds, or minutes, can he stay like this, I wondered, like last night, lying in bed, his gaze focused somewhere far away from me, his bloated hand, so rough, squeezing my tits, perhaps, it occurred to me now, because he preferred not to see them. I'd helped him to undress me, he'd hurried me on, he'd pulled off my knickers with one tug, and there I was, for the taking. He stared out of the corner of his eye at the tufts of curly hair covering my sex, and I directed one of his hands down there, he let me do it, but he didn't touch me, or stroke me, or rub me, he let his hand drop, like someone covering a hole so that nothing gets in or out. There he was, immobile, for a long time, and I didn't dare to take his clothes off as I had planned. I was falling into a deep sleep and he had to cover me with the blanket and switch off the bedside lamp.

Just like yesterday, Jaime didn't move. I took the charged glass, lingering for an instant with my fingertips brushing his rough hands, wide and paw-like.

The short man Jaime had brought to do the barbecue and who'd sat down to eat with us without a word was
stretched out in the shade a few metres away. He was snooz-
ing, belly-up, his forehead marked with charcoal.

I go back by train. Jaime drops me at the Luján bus station.
I soon find out that an unexpected transport strike has just
been called, that the last bus left at six thirty and that service
is suspended until further notice. An improvised handwritten sign is repeated in various ticket windows: *'No service'*. A
man tells me that if it were up to him he'd make the trip but
the thing is that on the motorway they might pelt the bus
with rocks. Or shoot at it, adds another man with his back
to us, playing solitaire on a computer. The next train leaves
in twenty minutes, says a voice from within. It's raining. I
approach the taxi rank and take the first of a long queue,
which gets me to the railway station in under five minutes.
The platform is filling with people, most of them students,
calming their nerves with cigarettes and increasingly rowdy
conversations. There are also workers, pensioners, women
with babies and a pair of drunks resting their elbows on a
hamburger stand. The train finally arrives, ten minutes late.
It's empty and I sit down by a window that won't shut. I swap
seats, but soon, when the train starts moving, the window
catch gives way and I have to hold it all through the journey to keep from getting wet. In the next compartment,
across the corridor, are four young seminary students, each
one younger than the next. Only one of them is dressed as
a priest. But there's no doubt, it's patently obvious that they

are a brotherhood. They chat, read and joke amongst themselves. The one in the cassock has a guitar case between his
legs. The carriage fills up, the atmosphere becomes tense.
The jolting of the train begins to lull me to sleep, until an
unexpected event draws my attention. It's not entirely clear
how or when the fight begins. First there's a struggle that
the darkness doesn't let me see fully. There are three or four
involved, boys and girls, pulling at each other's hair on the
platform of a very old station, while the doors of the train
are still open. There's a bicycle in the middle, someone slips,
someone else clings onto a wheel, kicking in the air. It's no
big deal, it's not serious, and yet it's enough to change the
course of the journey. The boy on the ground manages to
crawl onto the train, dragging the handlebars behind him.
The student priests fall silent, they observe the situation,
they question it with their eyes, slightly tense, but they don't
intervene. The doors close suddenly and the boy who made
it on board gradually composes himself. Those left on the
platform kick the chassis of the carriage and one of the boys,
or girls, launches a gob of spit that splats against the student
priests' window.

Initially, it's hard to tell whether the boy who got on the
train is the victim or the culprit. His face is flushed, he trem-
bles slightly, and, despite being a robust lad, he looks ready
to spill a few tears at any moment. There's no doubt that he's
the victim. With his gaze glued to the window, mortified,
he hides as best he can from the stares of those around him,
he rubs his mud-soiled hands, and discovers a small super-
ficial wound on his right palm, which he spends the rest of

the journey sucking. Occasionally, he bites his right thumb as well, whether to control the pain or because he's angry, I don't know. He wants time to pass more quickly.

As the minutes tick by, the glances that have been measuring him up, initially with apprehension, then with curiosity, and finally with compassion, give way to indifference and oblivion. Three or four stations further on, to bury the incident once and for all, one of the student priests decides to take out the guitar and, with some very rudimentary arpeggios, accompanies himself in a song in a strange form of Spanish that sounds rather antiquated, which gradually inspires the other young priests to join in with the chorus.

I arrived at Aída's at around half ten, without thinking too much about why I was going there, whether it was to pick up my belongings, to find out whether Beba had any news or even in the hope that Aída herself would be there to surprise me with some preposterous anecdote that would bring the whole thing to a close. I went up to the fourth floor and when I tried to open the door of the flat my key wouldn't even fit in the lock. I rang the bell a couple of times. Nothing, no response. I peeked through the gap next to the skirting board: complete darkness.

At the main door I came across the building manager, who was smoking with his back to me, a thin fishing rod under his arm. He wasn't surprised to see me, in either a good or a bad way. He signalled that he'd be back soon and reappeared with a sheet of paper folded in three that was addressed to me, with Friday's date and an official stamp. I read the heading. *Subject: Urgent service of process. National Court of Criminal Instruction . . .* It was a court summons for Monday morning at ten.

I start walking aimlessly, drifting. It's almost midnight and the city reeks of a collective hangover. *Kalton Family Hotel,* says an illuminated sign half a block from where I am. I head over to it. I ring the bell, a little man with a moustache sticks the top half of his body over the counter, weighs me up, slightly surprised, and eventually opens the door. It's no more than that, a typical family hotel, a solution.

'Just one night,' I say, 'just for today.'

'Twenty pesos for a private bathroom. Fifteen for shared.'

'Private bathroom,' I say, and the man is pleased.

Second floor, room twenty-seven, I find it hard to believe there are so many. I climb the stairs and walk from one end of the narrow corridor to the other, making the loose floorboards creak. There's no sign of anyone, they're all in their rooms, single men and women, families with children, couples, lovers: I can picture them all perfectly. The hallway is a war-zone, a violent crossroads of who knows how many televisions blaring all at once. Everyone against everyone else, the winners are those who dare to turn up the volume that bit more.

On the door of twenty-seven, the seven is missing. The room is essentially a giant bed enclosed in a kind of hole, a cement niche painted red. It's hellish, it's all there is. The carpet is flooded, as is my private bathroom. I'm too exhausted to ask to change rooms.

I lie down and the weight of my body forces the different lumps filling the mattress to spread around me. It's like lying on a ball of uncooked dough. At least the bedside lamp works. I stretch out my arm, open the drawer of the bedside table and grab the only thing that's in it, a slim book with a very soft cover that says on the front in Portuguese, imprinted in gold capitals: *New Testament.* And at the bottom: *Free distribution.* I let it fall open: *John 9:1.* I read in a low voice:

'*As he went along, he saw a man blind from birth. His disciples asked him, "Rabbi, who sinned, this man or his parents, that he was born blind?"*

'*"Neither this man nor his parents sinned," said Jesus, "but this happened so that the works of God might be displayed in him. As long as it is day, we must do the works of him who sent me. Night is coming, when no one can work. While I am in the world, I am the light of the world."*

'*After saying this, he spit on the ground, made some mud with the saliva, and put it on the man's eyes. "Go," he told him, "wash in the pool of Siloam" (this word means "Sent"). So the man went and washed, and came home seeing.*'

EIGHT

Very early on Monday. I'm woken by a chorus of strange noises from inside and outside the hotel. It's a grey morning. I call the surgery and leave a message saying that I'll be there around eleven.

'I've got some urgent business to take care of,' that's what I say.

I dial Aída's number to make some kind of arrangement with Beba to pick up the rest of my things. I try three times, and each time the phone rings out. Aída's voice, recorded on the machine, no longer answers. Things are moving quickly.

The courthouse is a labyrinth of corridors. I keep returning to the same place, the wrong place: a desk where a policewoman sits in front of a very thick book. By this stage, she doesn't even ask to see my ID before letting me go any further, as she did the first few times.

'Which office are you looking for, love?' she asks reluctantly, knowing that all of us here are after some office or other. She shows me where to go, it's a bit more difficult than I had thought. None of the notions I had about the legal system are as fantastical as the reality.

Finally I come to the office indicated on the summons.

I make my presence known at the window. It's really a door split into two. I'm told to wait in the corridor, they'll call me. It takes fifteen minutes. People circulate around me, some in a hurry, some taciturn, alone or in groups of two or three, and I catch murmured snatches of a conversation already in full flow, all inference and tainted dialogue, unending. Almost all carry files under their arms: lawsuits, documents, warrants, statements, expert reports. A young couple and an older man exit from a door at the side. The couple seem uncomfortable, embarrassed. Whatever the reason for their summons, they hadn't thought it would go this far. The man, meanwhile, puffs out his cheeks, holding back a smile.

My name is called.

'Bernardo Yasky, court clerk,' is how he introduces himself.

He's young, with very thick eyebrows, neither fat nor thin, neither ugly nor handsome, with smooth skin and stubby hands. He doesn't make eye contact for a single second during the half hour I'm there. He's wearing a white shirt with thin blue and grey stripes, and a regulation black tie. His chest is very hairy, lots of little black curls showing through his shirt.

I tell him everything, almost exactly, while he types from memory, not watching the screen, his hands agile, as if they'd broken away from the rest of his body. He types and smokes. Afterwards, without looking at me, he reads out my statement.

Finally, he asks if I want to add anything. No, it's fine like that. Then, at top speed, he finishes combining my words with the legal forms. Done, he says and wheels his chair over to the printer. He hurries the pages, pulling them out before they're quite ready, and lays them in front of me as if this were a hand of poker and these were my cards. The guy stretches out his legs beneath the desk and unintentionally kicks my ankle with the toe of his shoe. I jump, I wasn't expecting it and he over-apologises.

But he doesn't draw back his legs, and once or twice I feel them brush mine again, inadvertently. As he marks the places where I have to sign with a faint pencil cross, he says, without lifting his eyes from the papers, almost smiling:

'I'm rather clumsy.'

I read the last paragraph before signing: (. . .) *I SWEAR under penalty of perjury that I have told the truth to the best of my knowledge and belief in response to the questions I have been asked*. I sign, doubtfully.

Afterwards, next to the door, imprisoned between two high shelves filled to the brim with boxes that could land on top of us at any moment, we say goodbye with a handshake. He has the last word: We'll probably summons you again, he says, and releases my hand.

Since I finished somewhat earlier than expected, I

decide to walk to the surgery to kill time. I think about Aída, I go over my statement in my mind. At no point did I lie.

I arrive at the surgery and, behind the counter, a girl I've never seen before mistakes me for a client. I tell her who I am and her smile tightens slightly. From the till, she removes an envelope with my name on it. It's the owner's handwriting, I know it well. She says she's sorry, but she has to sack me, she says I left her no alternative. In fact, she's not sacking me, she's asking me not to complicate things and to send her my resignation. She's also left me a bit of money, compensation I suppose.

My gaze moves swiftly across this animal world that was mine for almost six months. I thank the girl by raising a hand, leaving the letter on the counter. She purses her lips and raises her shoulders, apologising for something that wasn't her doing. She seems happy with her new job. I wonder whether I ought to give her some practical advice.

I spend the next few days and nights in the Hotel Kalton. The night watchman gets me a television in return for a tip. I eat in bed, I watch all the programmes and when I get bored I turn to the Brazilian bible, which I read in parts, at random, wherever it falls open. I understand Portuguese much better than I thought I did. It's a pleasing language, full of the sounds of the wind. I've been paid up to and including Friday, so I just let myself be.

NINE

On Saturday, I take the train again and I'm in Open Door before midday. I was in two minds about whether to bring the Brazilian bible with me, but no, why would I need it.

I arrive at the house on foot, I don't have a single peso left, not even enough for the bus. It feels like a long way. Jaime was expecting to see me sooner, or at least to hear from me.

'I couldn't come any earlier, I had a legal matter to take care of,' I say and he doesn't show any interest in finding out what.

The first thing I do is to examine the other Jaime, who has improved considerably. It shows in the whites of his eyes, which are much livelier, and in the rhythm of his breathing. Jaime asks whether he could get better by himself. With difficulty, I reply.

Why did I come? I don't question myself, Jaime asks me even less. We start preparing a meal. We both happen to be very hungry. The radio is loud: there's a tacit agreement not to speak.

Later, after lunch, I tell Jaime about Aída. My story lasts the time it takes for him to roll and smoke three of his cigarettes. The kitchen reeks of smoke.

'You must be sad,' he says, or asks. With Jaime, it's hard to tell.

When we take our siesta, Jaime offers me his bed again but this time he doesn't ask my permission to lie down next to me. He's less inhibited and takes advantage of the first brush of contact to stroke my back underneath my blouse. He kicks off his boots, snorting. I help him to undress, and take off my own clothes. Before I know it, he's inside me. For a few minutes. He doesn't leave me time for anything.

We sleep our siesta with our backs to each other. The sheets smell clean, Jaime must have changed them with me in mind. Or perhaps not, it could just be a coincidence. It's my first siesta for a long time. I enjoy it, although the silence unsettles me at times.

When I open my eyes, it's already night-time. Jaime is still aroused. He climbs on top of me again. This time he grips the headboard with both hands, his nose scraping the wall. He moves like an animal. I try to take pleasure from it. At times I even succeed. His penis slips out and I feel it colliding against the inside of my thighs. It struggles, almost manages to enter again but immediately slides out, ending up limp with the effort. I cool off, I become dry. I wait for him to sort himself out with his hand, for him to wet his fingers with saliva and pass them over my lips. But it would seem that Jaime doesn't know about that sort of thing, even less that he wants to find out. He persists. My face is squashed up against his solid, hairy chest. It's no use, I end up having to make way with my own hand. I guide him. He's a terrible lover, with no technique.

On Sunday, Jaime wakes up with a fever. A relentless, country fever. He says it's nothing, that it will soon pass. I touch his forehead with my palm. It's boiling.

Some five hundred metres from the house, there's a small shop. Jaime asks me to go and buy some coarse salt to make him a steam bath. He tells me to take the pick-up. I say I'd prefer to walk. The road is full of potholes, enclosed by two barbed-wire fences, three wires high on the right and four on the left. It's half twelve and the sun, close to its zenith, prevents me from seeing things as they really are. The shop door is a curtain of rubber strips which I pull aside in order to pass through. There's no one there. Hello, I say, but there's no answer.

I retreat and, at the entrance, I clap my hands together. Still no response. I clap again, harder this time, and I hear the patter of small, reluctant, dawdling footsteps. The first thing I see is not that pair of tiny feet, with skin like dirty porcelain; instead it's the dust they raise as they drag along. The feet stop and I hear a soft breath close behind me.

I raise my head and have to lean slightly to see a round, flushed face, the forehead covered in pimples. It's a girl, somewhere between thirteen and sixteen; at that age you can never tell.

'We're closed,' she says, 'we open again at four.'

Silence. Neither of us moves from our position: I remain in the shade, she's in the sun. I don't know what to say, nor does she and, almost in unison, we shrug, hers apologetic, mine regretful. But I can tell that she likes me, or that she's bored, or something like that, because she changes her mind straight away.

'Do you need much?'

'A packet of coarse salt.'

'Come in,' says the girl, and enters the shop, raising more dust. I follow her, a metre behind. Inside, it's cool and dimly lit, ideal to rest my eyes and my head for a while, worn out as they are from so much sun. A light, crystalline dust with a taste of pollen envelops the atmosphere. It's there and it's not there, I can feel it, but I can't see it, like a spent cloud at ground level.

It's a typical general supply shop, but quite a bit smaller and much poorer than those that you still see in some villages, imitating those of days gone by. Even so, despite its precarious construction, it has that characteristic spirit of a cosmic market that conveys a sense of powerful abundance. Against the back wall, behind the counter, shelves reach to the roof, fashioned from piles of bricks and planks of wood, forming niches of different sizes in which the less usual merchandise is kept. It's not that the items are unusual in themselves, the odd thing is their coexistence. Their proximity to each other makes them absurd. There are brooms, flippers, bulk and bagged flour, candles, nails, screws, nuts, whips, household and garden tools, inflatable dolls, bundles of wood, balls, portable barbecues, lifejackets, two bicycle wheels, a cement mixer, noodles, two fishing rods with red floaters, bottles of gin, liqueurs and demijohns, an old mobile phone with a broken antenna, more balls, sunglasses, stale bread, three carrots, six potatoes, a tomato, various pairs of espadrilles hanging from a string of garlic, all together and in full view.

The girl climbed a high stepladder and took a moment to find the salt, which, in the end, she found by her hand.

'I don't serve very often,' she apologised, 'it's my dad and brother who work here.'

I watched her in silence and now that I could see her better, without the sun on her face, there was something in her gaze, in her precise hand gestures, that I couldn't put my finger on, something that made her rather unusual.

I asked her for a box of matches, just so that I could look at her a bit longer.

She had a slim back that contrasted with her hips, which were very developed for her age. She was wearing faded trousers, full of patches and mud stains.

'Anything else?' she asks and I stay quiet as long as I can, just for the sake of it, I want to see what she does. She gets nervous, glancing at me, she bites her lips until she ends up smiling. She reveals her teeth, very small and white, all the same size, like the matching pieces of a game. I pay for the salt and the matches and I'm pushing aside the plastic strips when I hear her voice again.

'You're not from round here, are you?'

'No, I'm not from round here. I'm passing through,' I say. It's about right.

The girl comes to the door and waves her hand vigorously, as if we were never to see each other again.

TEN

It's Monday morning and Jaime is feeling much better, although he still has a touch of fever. I prepare a mug of maté and take it to him in bed. It's best, we agree, that he doesn't go out until his temperature drops. I suggest calling a doctor, but he's almost annoyed by that. It's not serious enough to call a doctor, he says.

'Don't you have to go back?' Jaime asks, beginning to sense that I don't, and hurriedly adds:

'You don't need to worry about me.'

He asks me to go to the hospital to drop off some papers at the office. They're time-sheets, he explains without my asking and adds: So that I get paid. He gives me the keys of the pick-up and a few instructions about how to get there.

As I'm leaving, he stresses, in case I'm in any doubt:

'You can take all the time you want.'

•

I pull up in front of the barrier at the hospital entrance and wait my turn. The guards are registering a car that's leaving, checking the boot and confirming the identity of the people inside, they're very strict. It's like crossing a border in wartime.

One of the guards approaches, walkie-talkie in hand, and asks for my details. I fill out a form while the guy casts his eye over the back of the pick-up. His expression suggests that he has everything under control. He almost smiles at me and raises the barrier.

I'm met by a long drive of about eight hundred metres, shimmering in the sun's rays, tall trees like sentries on each side, leading to a roundabout with a pergola surrounded by palm trees at its centre. Road signs come into view at the end of the drive, to help visitors familiarise themselves. *Slow, Patients Crossing,* says the first, and further ahead: *Block 8 Sub-Acute Care and Surgery.* And in the middle distance I catch a glimpse of my first loonies, dressed in orange or blue. One passes close by, an enormous yellow rosary hanging round his neck.

I accidentally circle the roundabout twice, then park the truck next to the other cars, between the main building and a pleasant-looking kiosk with a tiled roof.

With Jaime's papers under my arm, I climb the wide steps that lead up to this kind of castle. Management to the right, administration to the left. I follow the arrow. I knock on the door and wait for a response. A pale-faced girl answers, her black hair in a bowl-cut, her white blouse buttoned to the neck. Catholic or trendy, I can't tell which. She is wearing a thin gold chain but whatever is hanging from it is hidden beneath the fabric. I give her the papers and she recognises them straight away. She smiles, touching the tip of her nose.

Outside, a day of brilliant sunshine beckons. I smoke a cigarette underneath the pergola. This place is incredible, it makes no sense.

Suddenly, out of nowhere, three guys appear. They come towards me. They walk close together, shoulder-to-shoulder. Denim jackets, black trousers, white trainers and sunglasses: from a distance they look identical, as if in uniform. They're loonies, I suppose, and yet they don't look like it, dressed like that, so streetwise. They approach, surrounding me. They don't seem surprised to see me. They ask me for a cigarette, I don't have any. So they try for a peso:

'Can you spare a peso?' they ask. Another no. They move on. One of them glances back at me and murmurs something that makes the others laugh.

It's after one o'clock when I get back to the farm. Jaime is in the kitchen making lunch, he looks much better.

'Good as new,' he exaggerates and asks happily: 'How did you get on at the loony bin?'

I tell him a bit about my impression of the place and ask him what's at the back, on the other side of the roundabout, where the three loonies emerged in their sunglasses, looking like three ordinary guys.

'Rehabilitation, drug addicts,' he says, his voice changed, as if he were talking about extra-terrestrials.

The phone rings. Jaime answers, it's for me.

'A Yasky,' he says, 'from the court.'

And in the five seconds before I take the receiver from him, a thousand suspicions pass through my mind. Most of them horrible.

'I need you to come to the Judicial Morgue at eight tomorrow,' Yasky says, without preamble. I don't know how to answer him, the idea leaves me frozen. He explains that he hasn't been able to contact Aída's aunt, who is the only family member they are aware of, so I'm the only suitable person to identify the body.

'Are you sure it's her?' I ask in a whisper.

'I'll expect you tomorrow,' answers Yasky.

I stand with the receiver still in my hand, shaken. I don't know how Yasky managed to get this number. Jaime complains because he doesn't like being disturbed by the phone while he's eating. I wonder where Beba could have got to.

That night, fear overtook me, and with fear came insomnia. I dream wakefully, lots of nightmares all together, each worse than the last. Aída appears in almost all of them. I wet the bed, I can't help it.

In the morning, Jaime asks me whether I want to bring my things here, to be more comfortable. Don't I need them? No, I tell him, I'm fine like this. Jaime insists. He says he could bring the pick-up and help me. I don't have any things, I say and he doesn't ask again.

ELEVEN

The Judicial Morgue is in Calle Viamonte, behind the School of Economic Sciences. I present myself at the entrance. A thin policeman tells me without looking at me that I have to wait. Until someone from the court arrives. I ask him whether he can't tell someone I'm here anyway. There's nothing to tell. He also asks me, this time to my face, still not looking me in the eye, but addressing me to my face, to wait in the street so as not to get in the way. I oblige.

Others who, like me, must be here to identify a corpse, file past under my nose: alone, in groups of two or three or four, depending on the circumstances, civilians or police officers, some hurried, some sorrowful, some embarrassed. Silent accomplices to the situation, some ignore me, while others look directly at me, by chance or on purpose, wondering: what is she doing? What's she waiting for? Who can have died?

An old woman with tinted tortoiseshell glasses, the kind that are coming back into fashion, gets out of a patrol car with the help of a fat man who takes her arm. He is wearing a suit and carrying a briefcase. She approaches in slow motion, pausing at a lamp post close to my shoulder to catch her breath. Wait here a moment, I'll be back in a tick, says the fat man, but the woman pays no attention to him. Very faint, fine lines cover her face, like a teenager who's been up all night. She exaggerates a noisy sigh, to attract my attention. I look at her. She's waiting anxiously for me to say something. She speaks first.

'This is hell. Could someone tell me when this damned summer is going to end? And they say that winter will be even worse. And to top it all . . .'

The old woman unfolds her arms to her sides, as far as her well-used joints allow, in a gesture of complaint. She takes a deep breath and continues.

'They tell me I've got to be strong because the body has decomposed quite a bit . . . it was in the flat for almost a week without them realising . . .'

The old woman leaves a deliberate, dramatic pause. Then she becomes anxious and speaks again, her voice scratchy and rather sinister:

'Apparently the poor thing suffocated on her own vomit,' she says and squeezes my wrist as if to say something else, something that she swallows at the last minute, when the fat man appears and takes her arm. The sun is burning my forehead, I feel ridiculous.

Yasky arrived forty-five minutes late. He apologises twice and adds laconically, by way of explanation:

'Such terrible weather.'

I don't understand how he can wear a jacket in this heat. A fat file is squeezed under his armpit, a lawsuit. I wonder what the brief could be.

The corridors of the morgue are much less gloomy than I expected. In fact, they're quite the opposite, a strange hybrid of a hospital and a university on a quiet day. The walls have been painted recently; they shine.

Yasky walks briskly, his fleshy body swaying, and I follow close behind. Now that I can see him properly, Yasky is just an ordinary guy, sometimes refined, sometimes distinctly average, the type who likes collecting things in his spare time, by era: stamps, vinyl records, pornography.

'We've been given an impossible case,' he reveals, without looking at me. 'Three bodies, no weapon, no motive. A whole family.'

We stop in front of a door with a bronze plaque with the word *Administration* marked out in relief. Yasky knocks twice, there's no immediate response. He turns slightly and contrives a kind of quick smile, out of obligation, or nerves. The door opens and the man who answers must be two metres tall, ginger from top to toe, an enormous head, his flat face peppered with a thousand freckles. His arms and cheeks are equally hefty. He must be about fifty and looks to me as though he has Irish roots. He takes no notice of me, but lets Yasky in and shuts the door. Five minutes later, it swings open and Yasky sticks out his head.

'There are a few formalities to take care of, we'll just be a moment,' he says and during this new wait, a question consumes my thoughts to the point of obsession. It's a question I haven't asked until now, a stupid question that doesn't change anything, but I can't help it. Was Aída looking at me as she fell?

Yasky comes out again, this time followed by the massive redhead who ignores me completely when I try to catch his eye to greet him. He's a sullen type. His freckles give him a candour that openly contrasts with his character.

This time Yasky and I walk next to each other, the ginger man leading the way, along the same corridor as far as a double door. The redhead lets us into a room with three trolleys welded to the floor and lots of drawers with handles along the far wall. The atmosphere is cool, much more agreeable than outside. On the trolley to the right, the nearest to the door, there is a shape, a body, its extremities protruding slightly, covered by a polythene sheet. The first thing I see is a pair of feet, not yet entirely blue, falling to either side, thoroughly dead. And I find it hard to believe that these are Aída's feet.

Yasky gestures for me to follow him. We position ourselves on either side of the trolley. The man talks to Yasky, but it's aimed at me:

'The body isn't in very good condition,' he says, taking his position at the head, like in the films. He moves unhurriedly, he knows the score, he's an expert in dealing with corpses, you can tell. For a few seconds, Yasky and I just observe the out-stretched plastic. Aída comes to my mind, her long face, the prominent nose, the curly hair, caressing me with moist hands, and then moaning, then smoking.

'When you're ready,' the man says to both of us, as if Yasky were part of the family. Yasky deflects the question to me with his eyes, nodding slightly, and I must make some gesture that the other man takes as agreement because he whips back the sheet in one swipe, without warning, revealing much more of the body than is necessary, as far as the middle of the abdomen: the skin is opaque, the eyelids sealed, the mouth slightly open, expressionless, her parts seem put together by force, as if in a collage, the breasts falling to either side like the feet, the hair like dried seaweed.

I shake my head and avert my gaze, swallowing a lot of saliva.

'Are you sure?' asks Yasky, a bit hoarsely.

'Completely sure,' I reply and I don't know why I add: 'Nothing like her.'

The ginger giant wants to give me another chance and instead of hurrying, he takes his time covering up the unknown woman's head. I can't help looking at her again: a corpse, the first I've ever seen close up, so horrible and so simple, no mystery. It's not so bad. How many times have I seen living beings who are much more broken? In my mind's eye, I can conjure up dead animals of all species. I thought that this would be different, but no, it's the same. I feel strong, I've just faced death in flesh and bone and I'm still standing, whole and unaffected. A morbid fascination grips me, I want to see more, but the body is covered again and Yasky is following the giant to the door. Did I disappoint them?

The same scene is repeated: Yasky and the other guy disappear into the office again, I remain outside. Perhaps

Aída is locked in one of the drawers, unable to say: Here I am. Five, ten minutes go by, I get bored. I wander off, away from the exit, to see what I find. There's not a soul to be seen. On both sides of the corridor there are further doors, all closed and nameless. What do morgue employees do? Talk on the phone, do the filing, organise meetings, make plans for the weekend, like normal public servants. At a corner, where the corridor turns and narrows, there's a coffee machine. I slot in two coins and press a button: espresso, medium-sweet. The machine launches into action. Across the screen runs the word: *Preparing*. I wait with folded arms. Behind me a door opens and closes. I turn round and a boy with a knot of snakes tattooed on his forearms comes and stands next to me. Hi, he says and I notice how the open jaws of the snakes bite at his wrists. I return his greeting and it strikes me that the morgue is like a small village where everyone knows each other and an outsider like me has to pretend to belong to the tribe. The only thing I can think of to say is that it's very hot today. Yes, he responds enthusiastically and adds: And the air conditioning isn't working. The machine announces that my coffee is ready. *Preparation complete*, it says. I grab my cup and I don't know whether to wait for him to get his. Coffee makes me feel the heat less, he says and explains: It must be because the body heats up as well and the temperatures match. I don't know what to say.

Yasky appears at the other end of the corridor and beckons me. I raise my hand to say goodbye to the boy, he smiles at me, and only now do I see a piercing at the tip of his tongue.

Yasky has gone on ahead, he's waiting for me on the pavement, blocking the sun with one of his files. He's perspiring all over.

'I'm very sorry,' he says, 'these things happen sometimes. That's why this place exists.'

Everything seems to indicate that we're about to say goodbye. Before we do, I decide to ask:

'I'm curious about something. That woman, where did you find her?'

'At the bottom of the river, at the foot of the bridge.'

Yasky hails a taxi.

'I'll keep you informed, as soon as there's any more news.'

I still have a lot of questions, but I'll keep them for another time. It's so hot I could die.

TWELVE

The last weekend in February was the end of the carnival. We ate early, lentil stew, which I made myself and turned out a lot better than I expected. Exquisite, said Jaime after the first mouthful and he devoured the rest in one go.

As he did every day, Jaime started talking about the horse. It was his favourite subject, his only subject. Over the last few days, the other Jaime had made a noticeable improvement, it was difficult to explain. And, even though the nodules were still there, they'd magically decreased in size. Jaime fantasised about riding him again.

It's a miracle, he was saying, and the animal looked at him with his enormous eyes, with a mixture of helplessness and scepticism. Jaime repeated the word, with all the excitement of someone who suddenly believes in miracles for the first time.

'It's carnival,' I say presently, to interrupt him, 'let's go along for a bit and see what's happening.'

Jaime didn't refuse, but he didn't say yes either. He crushed his half-smoked cigarette into his plate next to the scraps of food and went to put on his boots straight away. He was an odd man, almost always decent, but he would change suddenly and become terse, ill-humoured. I was getting to know him.

I stuck my head out onto the veranda. A light, slanting drizzle was falling, swirling about to form thousands of razor-sharp droplets. Like fake carnival snow. Jaime brought the pick-up right to the door so that I wouldn't get wet. On the way to the village we didn't say anything, silenced by the thrum of the engine, or by the excitement of zigzagging over the wet mud to leave fresh tracks.

The *fiesta* took up five blocks on Avenida Cabred, the heart of the village. First of all, there was a parade of floats, each recognisable by the sound of their chosen anthem, repeated ad nauseam on loudspeakers. Each song played over the next, composing a kind of diabolical meta-melody. The floats were themed. Girls in dresses of fake sequins danced on top, making the rickety structures tremble. It was impossible not to think an accident would happen at any moment.

Alongside the floats passed jugglers, flame throwers, a giant caterpillar, the young and the young-at-heart exchanging jets of foam sprayed from bottles in the shape of Rey Momo the carnival king, a gaggle of internees from the hospital wearing unrecognisable costumes, families, single men and women, the two village transvestites and a small group of inoffensive drunks at the tail of the parade. Jaime parked the truck widthways across the street, parallel to the railway tracks, right in front of the abandoned silos at the entrance to the village. All kinds of vehicles had sneaked in behind the endlessly circulating floats: motorbikes, cars, a fire engine, sulkies and a cloud of bicycles that entered and exited the darkness like swift ghosts. Jaime bought a couple of cans of beer and we sat on the pavement, our legs hanging down into the ditch. And even though I was what you would call a recent arrival, some faces, still mostly nameless, were becoming familiar to me.

At one point a row broke out and Jaime became uneasy. We couldn't see much, but from a distance it appeared that two guys were about to come to blows. We moved closer and recognised Boca from behind, throwing himself on top of someone else who stumbled. Jaime signalled for me to stay where I was and pushed his way through the crowd, broke the circle of goading onlookers and shook Boca by the shoulder. It took him a good while to cool Boca down, all the blood had risen to his head and his gin-breath reached across the street. Jaime's intervention wasn't well received by a public hungry for a fight but you could tell that the other man, Boca's rival, wasn't entirely sure about fighting anyway because he didn't protest the matter for a single second.

Boca calmed down and at once acted as if nothing had happened. He talked a lot, we understood very little. He kept repeating that carnivals were old-fashioned.

'There's too much noise here,' he said at one point, fixing us with his tiny eyes. Jaime shrugged and I smiled.

Boca proposed going to buy more beer. Jaime stood up and gestured for me to go with him. I'll wait for you here, I said and Jaime smiled at me in the way that boyfriends do when they're parting from a girlfriend they've just started seeing.

The drizzle persisted, still swirling, still with thousands of tiny drops of moisture pricking at my cheeks. Everything seemed so strange to me, so new and fleeting. It was a bit like being on holiday, visiting a distant relative, the kind you never miss but who seem indispensable when they are close by.

Suddenly, a small hand rested on my shoulder. I jumped slightly and turned my head at once to see who it belonged to. It was Eloísa, the girl from the shop, who was already moving away with short steps, surrounded by other girls, looking at me out of the corner of her eye, with a mocking or conspiratorial little laugh, I never knew which.

I lay down on the wet grass, closed my eyes and Aída's face came into my mind, blurred by the smoke of the cigarette she calmly inhaled and exhaled. I began to drop off.

Boca's booming voice returned me to what was left of the carnival. Jaime sat down at my side, happy to find that his girl was still there. We shared a final can of beer, while Boca resumed his monologue. He was no longer talking about the carnival, now he was saying something about some guy who swore he'd seen a flying saucer in a nearby field.

THIRTEEN

Jaime and Boca had gone out early to buy building materials. It was a day of clear blue skies and fluffy, starched clouds. I was washing down the veranda when the telephone rang. Yasky's voice trembled slightly, it was hoarse, unclear.

'No, there's nothing new,' he says and pauses before continuing. 'It was just that, I wanted to let you know, I thought you'd be waiting . . . I'll call again when I have some news.'

That was it.

I continued mopping the veranda tiles until I couldn't go on and I lay down on the grass. Lying like this, my hands scratching at the dirt, my eyes duelling with the harsh rays of the sun, as if I were somewhere else, I let myself be taken by a delicious lethargy, which is violently interrupted by a sharp jolt that shakes me so hard I'm lifted a couple of millimetres off the ground. A powerful blow from within the earth. The echo of the tremor lasts for a few seconds. Then it fades, without explanation.

At lunchtime, Boca took over the barbecue again. I stayed with him for a while as he prepared the fire. A boy of about twelve or thirteen, with curly hair and a big mole at the base of his nose, was loitering around us. He kicked at broken pieces of brick with a grumpy face. He was entertaining himself in his own way. Later on I found out that his name was Martín and that he was Boca's nephew.

Although it was autumn the midday sun still warmed the skin. Boca was talking about the different cuts of beef, his hands smudged with charcoal, his eyes red as usual.

'Are you a believer?' he asked suddenly. Since I didn't know how to reply, he hunched his shoulders, pursed his lips and arched his eyebrows, all at the same time, but he didn't say anything else.

After eating, I started raking the path that leads from the house to the stable. When I opened the stable door I had a bad premonition. A short-lived premonition. The other Jaime was sprawled out, his head crushed against the back wall, his gums on view, tail mingling with the straw. The horse's eyes said it all: death had arrived suddenly.

Jaime didn't react immediately. He spent the rest of the afternoon and a good part of the night playing cards with Boca. They emptied a whole bottle of gin between them. I came and went, from the bedroom to the kitchen, I slept a bit and played a few hands when one or other of them went to the bathroom or needed a rest. A couple of times, Jaime left the house to go and see his horse. The first time he went alone, the second, Boca and I accompanied him. We dragged the animal outside, pulling him by a rope tied to his back legs. We took him as far as the mill. Jaime didn't seem to have taken it in, he was talking about buying a new scythe and about a loony who hid amongst the bushes at the plant nursery and made Jaime almost crap himself with fear when he appeared. Boca listened to him, drunker than ever. I watched them in silence, thinking that there's no such thing as miracles.

At one point, Jaime mentioned something about the stable, he said it was going to be left empty now, but he didn't make any direct reference to the animal. And that was the other Jaime's wake: in the open air and with lots of alcohol.

My eyes open in the middle of the night and, with less of a shock than the first few times, I find the bronze crucifix suspended in the air. A dusty, yellowish light forms its outline. It no longer seems as sordid to me, nor as suffocating as it used to. Now that I know it, it's inoffensive, necessary, in keeping with this rickety iron bedstead that squeaks when I try to make myself comfortable, and with all the rest, the vast doors, the cold floors, the marbled kitchen table, the broken bathroom tiles, every corner of the house frozen in time, the splintered shelves in the wardrobe, the earthenware pots, the bordered tablecloths, all the old stuff, Jaime, snoring at my side, and the mosquito nets. All of which brings me a new and unfamiliar peace.

The following morning, Boca and Jaime are talking in the kitchen. It doesn't look like they've been to bed at all. Boca says that the best thing would be to burn him, then bury the ashes somewhere. Cremate him, corrects Jaime. It sounds logical; a normal burial would be a colossal effort. Jaime doesn't seem convinced but he eventually accepts the solution and they decide to organise the bonfire for that same night. For the ceremony, Jaime invites his brother Héctor, who lives in Luján.

I spend the whole afternoon in bed, facing the ceiling. On the wardrobe, under some thick, moth-eaten blankets, there are two identical boxes, flat and round. I climb onto a chair to find out what's in them. The first one is empty, or practically empty. When I lift it up, a couple of mothballs rattle about inside. In the other, there are two books, a bundle of handwritten sheets of paper, a couple of faded photos and some loose locks of dark brown hair.

Later that day, I ask Jaime about the boxes.

'They've always been there,' he says and I can see that he's never had any reason to move them.

As the afternoon light was dying, Héctor arrived in his old pick-up, with his wife Marta and their twin sons. Nobody really asked what I was doing there, I was just another one of the family. Boca dug a groove around the horse to contain the fire. The boys accompanied me to the woods to collect dry logs and branches. Marta stayed in the house preparing the meal. Jaime and Héctor took charge of arranging the wood, creating a kind of primitive shack that caged the animal. At around ten we reconvened to start the bonfire. Jaime seemed to prepare himself to say a few words but he swallowed them and, without preamble, lit the fire at its four cardinal points, starting at the south and finishing in the west. At first, the fire didn't take properly, so Boca tried to revive it by dousing the wood with spurts of kerosene.

When we had eaten, the flames were still very high and the other Jaime was invisible. The twins played with the embers using lit branches as sparklers. Afterwards, they fell asleep, shoulder-to-shoulder. Boca drank all the wine again. Héctor told Jaime all about his projects, country stuff. I bored myself talking to Marta until she got bored of me.

There was much more left of the horse than we expected. Instead of ashes we found a heavy jumble of long bones, not entirely bare, which filled a pit the size of a small child behind the stable.

FOURTEEN

Skirting the fence, I spend the afternoon kicking pine cones. Behind the row of poplars, so that Jaime can't see me. I told him I was going shopping in Luján.

'And what do you need to get?' he asked.

'Women's stuff,' I answered in jest, but he didn't laugh. He was wondering what kind of stuff that might be.

The sky splits into almost perfectly equal bands, over where the sun is going to disappear. A whole spectrum of pastel colours. I'm beginning to lose count of all the afternoons I've already spent here.

I'm walking with my head down, in search of new pine cones to kick, so I jump when I hear a timid hello close by. It's Eloísa, the girl from the shop. Hi, I say and her eyes dart all over the place. Under her arm, she's carrying a rolled-up burlap bag. She's wearing a buttoned blouse patterned with tiny bunches of flowers, yellow, red and white, rococo style, and a black bra, which is very see-through, making her diminutive tits more pronounced.

'I'm going mulberry picking. Want to come?' she says. 'They're the last of the season, after these there won't be any more until October.'

We walk next to each other, my legs shrouded in denim, hers covered to the knee by a kilt, school uniform, I assume.

'Once, when I was little, I ate so many that I had a fever for at least a week,' says Eloísa and laughs, deliberately dragging her trainers. A cloud of dust follows us.

At the end of the road, Eloísa ducks and slips through a tiny gap between the strands of barbed wire that separate Jaime's land from the polo field. I catch a glimpse of her knickers. I squeeze through, with a bit of a struggle. Eloísa laughs again.

On the left, between two trees interlacing at their crowns, a narrow path begins, plunging to a practically dry stream. Momentum sends us flying down. It's outright forest. Eloísa runs in front of me, raising the burlap bag above her head as if it were a mini parachute.

'We need to go higher, the branches down here have already been picked, they're the easiest to reach. Are you game?'

We climbed the tree, and it felt a bit as though we'd always been doing this. We ate red mulberries, those that were left, which weren't many.

'Do you have a boyfriend?'

'Something like that.'

'And where does he live?'

'There,' I say, pointing at the farm. Eloísa laughs at Jaime and at me. She imagines us together.

'But he's an old man,' she says and I don't know how to respond. I cough. Eloísa doesn't insist but she asks me lots of other questions, whatever comes into her head. I answer some, others, most of them, she answers herself.

Where are you from? Do you like it here? Aren't you bored? What about your friends? Do you smoke? How long are you going to stay? You're joking about the old man, aren't you? Have you ever eaten white mulberries? What about medlars? Would you like to try them?

She speaks rapidly, all at once, while she destroys a rotten mulberry between her finger tips. Her nails are bitten, painted a long time ago with a child's varnish. Now she falls silent and without meaning to, in trying to reach some difficult mulberries, she shows me her knickers again. I can't help it, I want to touch her.

We said goodbye a few steps from the gate, with the night on top of us. First, we tried to cross the stream to pick some little wild tomatoes that were visible from the other side. But Eloísa slipped and fell in the water. She was drenched.

'If you like, another day we could go and see if there are any figs left on the other side of the polo field,' she said to me in the almost darkness.

FIFTEEN

Jaime wakes up feverish again. He stays in bed all day, against his will. I make him drink lots of water and wrap him up well so that he sweats. He says he must have something because he's not the kind to fall ill easily. I tell him it could be a virus, that nowadays they're very resistant and that he'll have to be patient. He looks at me distrustfully.

Amongst the books that I found in the round boxes on top of the wardrobe was one in French: *En Argentine, De Buenos Aires au Grand Chaco*, written by a certain Jules Huret, and published in Paris in 1911. On the second page, in smudged black ink, I can just about make out a dedication in Spanish: *To Dr Domingo Cabred, great visionary and Creole.* It is signed Jules Huret, Paris, Oct '11.

At first glance it seems to be a kind of travelogue by a Frenchman who visited Argentina at the beginning of the twentieth century. The contents page lists several chapters devoted to Buenos Aires, its various neighbourhoods, its institutions and, of course, its people, *los porteños*. Further on, it talks about the countryside. What follows is an excursion in caravan to the north of the country, stopping at Tucumán, Jujuy, Salta, the Chaco Austral, the forest of El Impenetrable, Corrientes, the upper Paraná, Misiones, the Iguazú Falls, the Jesuit ruins and the Israeli colonies in Entre Ríos. I read the topics listed on the contents page several times and imagine a strange fascination in the eyes of this European confronted by so many things so far from home. In one of the initial chapters, entitled *'Les criminaux et les fous'*, I discover a section on Open Door and Cabred. I look for the page but I needn't have bothered, I can barely understand it at all.

That same afternoon I make a trip to the Open Door library with Huret's book under my arm.

It must be about thirty blocks, half of them unpaved, half of them tarmacked. The village is at its best, full of life. A man carrying a pair of spurs shows me how to get there. Just before the level crossing, I turn right, pass the bar with the pool tables where they were selling beer on the day of the carnival, I walk a few more metres and there I am.

Behind the desk, Brenda, the librarian, attends to me, a village girl with hair down to her waist. I tell her that I'm looking for a French translator and she freezes as though I've insulted her. I tell her what it's about. She pinches her lips and finally brings herself to speak. She tells me that she has quite passable French. A foreign language was obligatory at school and she never liked English much. But she's never translated anything, she adds with a touch of panic. I show her Huret's book, in particular the part devoted to Open Door.

She took an immediate interest. She examined the book with great delicacy, treating each page as if it were about to break. She ran her eyes along the lines, murmuring slightly to herself, nodding her head from time to time. She stayed like that for about five minutes, without saying a word to me. In the meantime, I entertained myself by leafing through a magazine that was on her desk. It was published locally, handmade and distributed free. The main article was about the history of Open Door, it was the second instalment. There were some photographs, the first villagers, the arrival of the train, a *fiesta* in the barn, all black and white.

'This is a very valuable book,' Brenda said finally and showed me the last page, which stated that only ten unique numbered copies had been printed, on Japanese paper. I was impressed.

'And why do you want to get it translated?' she wanted to know.

'Out of curiosity,' I replied and Brenda wasn't entirely satisfied with my answer. 'Do you fancy doing it?'

Brenda raised her shoulders, smiled and I saw that she did, that she would give it a try. I left the book with her. As we said goodbye, because she came with me to the door, I saw that her right leg ended in a stump and that she was in a wheelchair. I hid my surprise and thanked her. We agreed that I would call the following week.

By night-time Jaime's fever had dropped a bit but he was still under the weather. I made him some broth and took it to him in bed. To distract him, I tell him about my trip to the library, about Brenda, and about what I learned of the history of Open Door. Jaime drinks his soup and, with every sip, produces a terrifying sound like broken turbines. I ask him how it was that Huret's book, with its dedication to Cabred, had ended up in his possession. He tells me that it's not his book. That he doesn't read books.

Very early, we are woken by the telephone. We leave it ringing, but it persists and I have to get up to answer it. It's Yasky, from the court. He says that today, as soon as possible, I have to attend the morgue again.

I don't tell him this, but the truth is that I'm starting to forget about Aída. I don't know whether to feel guilty. The appointment is for three in the afternoon. I wonder whether this time it will be her. Before hanging up, Yasky apologises.

I tell Jaime, who is slightly annoyed. He doesn't understand how it can be so difficult to find a body. A body, he repeats.

Eloísa is gesturing to me from the gate. I gesture back for her to come in, but she stays where she is, waving her hand. I go over to her. I want to talk to you, she says and takes me along a path I've never been on, through the woods, as far as a fig tree, full to bursting, which we relieve of its fruit until we're sated. Eloísa holds the figs by the base and with her tongue licks the sweet, sticky milk, before opening and devouring them. Her lips shine. She tells me that the other day a boy asked her to take her clothes off, after school one afternoon, near here.

'And I got naked, I was bad,' I don't know if she's expecting me to comment. She stares at me, her eyes wide, it seems as though she's going to touch me, but she changes her mind.

'Was I bad?' This time she's definitely asking me.

It's almost two o'clock, I've got to go. Jaime is waiting to take me to the morgue. He insisted on coming with me, even though he isn't completely better. But Eloísa keeps me, she ensnares my eyes. She says that I have very white skin. She says it so that she can touch me, to see if it really is that white. She strokes my legs. Are you ticklish? I don't answer. She continues, and I laugh. And then, taking advantage of my distraction, she moves her face close to mine and gives me a dry kiss at the edge of my mouth, almost without meaning to, innocent. Then she becomes serious, she remembers something:

'What about you? Have you taken your clothes off in front of many boys?'

In the city, Jaime drives the same way he does in the country. We are repeatedly hurried on by blasting horns. I get out at the door of the morgue and Jaime goes to look for somewhere to park. This time Yasky is punctual. He seems impatient. We say hello quickly and take the same route as before. It's strange, I'm starting to feel secure in this place, fearless. We come across new faces, but there is still the same hubbub, subdued because of the proximity of dead bodies. Again, the Irish-looking man receives us. Yasky leaves us alone for a moment, he's forgotten to make an urgent call. The man shows me into his office. He offers me coffee. I accept. On the back wall, behind the desk, there is a poster of a snowy volcano reflected in a lake. The man picks a subject just to strike up a conversation. He's different, more amicable, he looks at me differently. He wants to know what I do, what my job is. I find it hard to believe, but he's trying to seduce me. I wonder whether it would occur to him to fuck me right here, surrounded by all those corpses. It sounds ridiculous, yet so natural, he's a womaniser like any other. Necrophilia is something else altogether. What must that be like, getting turned on by dead bodies?

Yasky opens the door just in time. He purses his lips, he can sense something. We repeat the same ritual as before but it's quicker this time. We take our places. We're a team. The body is uncovered for three seconds. I shake my head.

'This isn't her either,' I say, thinking that at least she's more like her than the first one was. Yasky is embarrassed, the other man almost laughs.

SIXTEEN

Not everyone says Open Door in the same way. Some say *Open* Door, others Open *Door*. Eloísa says *Open* Door, Boca and Jaime say Open *Door*. I haven't decided yet. It depends on the moment and who I'm with. In general I say *Open* Door, but to tell the truth I don't know which of the two I prefer.

The calendar hanging on the handle of the larder door is showing the wrong date. Nobody has pulled off the leaves since the second of March and we're up to the twentieth, or is it the nineteenth of April, I don't even know any more. I don't have anyone to ask. It's the middle of the night, there can only be a few hours until dawn. Jaime is snoring in the bedroom: it's not a strong snore, but it is persistent. It never switches off. At times it builds, moves from high-pitched to low, becomes angry, then abates before immediately catching breath and accelerating. When it's not a snore, it's a whistle, and when it's not whistling, it blows. In a certain way it

94

talks, it says things in that fundamental, universal language, difficult things, fragments of something that Jaime carries deep inside, in his guts, and releases at night without realising it, so that I can hear it and understand him a bit better, or so that I can start to despise him. I'm wide awake and more inclined to hatred than to understanding.

Now, in the kitchen, I take sips of gin to help me sleep. Then I see this calendar that I've never noticed until today and whose leaves nobody has removed for a long time. I pull them off one by one, from the second of March to the nineteenth of April. I'm about screw all the days into a ball and throw it in the rubbish bin but a discovery stops me. On the back of each leaf is a phrase in quotation marks. They are signed by celebrities, writers, artists, philosophers, statesmen, men and women of note, at first glance a lot more men than women. Each is something along the lines of a motto with which to face the new day. Some are confused or badly translated, most suggest impractical behaviour, there are Chinese proverbs, Creole phrases, Bible verses, fragments of universal literature. One of the most frequently recurring themes is avarice. Another is the relationship between body and soul.

I keep two quotes, one for its ingenuity, the other because it made me think. The first is by Schopenhauer, or at least the calendar attributes it to him, and it says: '*Woman is an animal with long hair and short ideas.*' Horace puts his name to the other: '*Not to bring smoke from fire, but light from smoke.*' I love it, I don't know why.

SEVENTEEN

Jaime finally felt better and went back to work. He leaves at seven, returns for lunch, we sleep a siesta together and every now and then we make love. At around half four, he goes out again, not returning until eight. In the morning he does building work with Boca on one of the small farms or estates in the area. He plans the refurbishments, buys the materials and deals with clients, while Boca provides the manpower. After our siesta, he goes to the hospital.

My routine is much more sedentary. I sleep late, eat breakfast alone, do a bit of tidying, listen to the radio, have a bath and kill time until half twelve when I start cooking. I've started to live like a housewife, without quite realising it, instinctively. In the afternoons, I walk in the woods or go into town for a bit of distraction. On the way there or back, I often bump into Eloísa on the road. Yesterday she invited me to watch television.

'Do you want to come to mine to watch telly for a bit?

My brother and my folks aren't in, they went away for a few days,' she said.

Eloísa's house is attached to the shop, it's a kind of annex, accessed through a separate door. Straight away it's clear that it's a makeshift construction, the proportions are unusual and there are lots of spaces without any obvious use. There's a hole for the window, but the window isn't there: in its place is a wooden board that can be removed and replaced. The only glimpse of the outside world comes through the skylight in the bathroom. There are two bedrooms and a multi-purpose room that includes the kitchen. The television occupies the centre of the house; all the furniture is arranged around it. One of the walls, the first I see when I go in, is papered with an enormous map of the world that, judging from the darts stuck in some countries, also serves as a target board.

We are sitting on the sofa-bed, it must be about six in the evening. Eloísa tells me they have sixty-six channels, as she runs through them all from one end to the other, over and over. She doesn't seem to tire of it. She asks the same question repeatedly: Shall I stick with this one? She asks me, but answers herself because she immediately skips to the next channel. And suddenly, without explanation, she switches off the set, throwing the remote control onto the floor. She crosses her legs, hugging a cushion, and looks at me face-on with an anxious smile.

'Do you want a smoke?' she asks and, from a little wooden box painted with a cat, she removes a fat joint. 'Here, you light it. My brother has, like, six plants hidden behind the henhouse, so it's free here. He takes care of them like they're made of gold, but if you ask him, he'll give you all you want.'

Two drags each, the joint passes back and forth. Eloísa stretches out her legs and kicks off her trainers, spinning them through the air. I look at her sidelong, my head lolling against the back of the sofa. She looks me straight in the eye.

'Will you show me your tits?' she asks quietly and laughs loudly. She says it completely naturally, with impunity, she doesn't give me time to react. 'Go on, just for a second.'

I say nothing, neither no nor yes. I laugh along with her, I close my eyes for an instant and when I open them, Eloísa has her t-shirt rolled up with her tiny tits on show, upturned like two drops of water. Ready for me to examine her. She shrugs. She wants to know if I like them.

'They're very nice,' I say. Eloísa stretches out her legs, stroking my knees with the soles of her feet.

'Don't you want to touch them?' she asks but gives me no time to respond and touches them herself.

The rain began suddenly, with hail and everything. First, two claps of thunder made the walls of the house vibrate and immediately water began to pour down in torrents. The corrugated iron roof made a terrible noise, like bursts of machine gun fire.

'You can't even think about going out in this,' says Eloísa, frenetically changing channels again. 'You've got no chance in this rain, the road must be a river,' she insists. She's right. It's almost eight and Jaime must be about to get home.

'I've got to let him know,' I say.

The phone is in the shop so I have no choice but to go outside and walk round. I've barely crossed the threshold and I'm soaked from head to toe. I follow Eloísa's instructions to get into the shop but I struggle so much that I almost give up. There are three padlocks, each tougher than the last. I eventually manage to gain entry. I pick up the receiver and I might have known: the phone is dead.

When I returned to the house, Eloísa was out of sight. She called me from her bedroom and found me a towel to dry myself.

'I'd better lend you some clothes, or you'll catch cold straight away,' she said and undertook to undress me herself. First my boots, then my trousers, blouse and the rest.

'Are you cold?' asked Eloísa and, again, didn't let me answer. She wrapped me in the towel and stared at me. Then, first with one hand, then with both, she began to touch my breasts, without asking my permission. Making circles, squeezing them, pinching my nipples, she played, she enjoyed herself.

Then Eloísa turned on the television again and we ate an enormous bag of crisps, watching a quiz show. The rain continued to fall hard. There was no sense in thinking about going back.

Night fell and tiredness pushed us into bed. Without meaning to we embraced. Eloísa fell asleep immediately. I took a bit longer. On my back, with Eloísa's hair covering half my face, my head fills with green things that skim past quickly, green flashes of lightning, images, abstractions.

They are strange yet agreeable shapes. Eloísa smells so good.

I open my eyes at some point in the early hours. Somewhere between surprised and scared. After the rain, it has become intensely cold. I have to go back. Before I leave, Eloísa, pretending to be asleep, gives me a long kiss on the mouth.

I arrived at the house with my trousers muddied up to the knees. From the gate, I could see more lights than usual and I knew that Jaime was waiting up for me. He was in the kitchen, his arms folded, his eyes beginning to close. He didn't even have the strength to ask me what had happened, but I told him anyway. I told him that I'd been trapped by the rain. Jaime couldn't accept that Eloísa's phone didn't work when his functioned perfectly.

'You can't do this,' he was saying. 'You should have let me know somehow. I was thinking about calling the police.' He was exaggerating.

EIGHTEEN

How do I know that guy sitting on a bench next to the pergola with sunglasses and a can of Coke in his hand? I can't remember. He's a normal-looking guy, the kind you see everywhere. I know him from somewhere though.

Jaime parks the pick-up to one side of the kiosk.

'Come on,' he says, 'I'm going to show you something.'

Jaime gives me a brief tour of the hospital facilities: the bakery, the power plant, the various workshops for shoes, textiles and carpentry, but the thing that Jaime really wants to show me is the road that leads to the nursery, his place of work. It's incredible, I say, quite sincerely. At night, explains Jaime, it's pitch black. He also shows me the houses for permanent staff and the play park. It's a little village inside another.

Now Jaime hurries because he has some business to discuss in the office and it's nearly one o'clock, lunch hour. I follow him. We circle the pergola again and that man, who continues to intrigue me, is still there, his back to me. He doesn't see me; there's no way to find out who he is.

Jaime heads towards the door where I dropped off his papers the last time, but he carries on and raps his knuckles against a glass window at the side. A head appears immediately, the same girl whose style had confused me before, but with an unexpected addition: a ring in her nose. Jaime introduces us and she no longer disconcerts me once I find out that her name is Laica. Jaime tells Laica about my interest in the history of Open Door. It's an idle comment, unnecessary. Laica smiles without saying anything. I feel uncomfortable.

The midday sun hits my forehead, stunning me. I descend the stairs, facing the pergola. The loony bin is at my feet and I'm a bit like a tourist fresh off the train, who leaves the station and begins to discover a new city whose buildings, trees and streets convey the illusion of time stood still: the historic centre, the main square, the town hall, the church, the houses, and its people. I get a bit lost. I'm a new arrival. I skirt the roundabout and head down an endless road with a crowd of ancient eucalyptus on either side. I'm taking a bit of a chance. In the distance, two silhouettes are advancing rapidly towards me. They get bigger. I retrace my steps.

I take some more turns and come out at the back of the sports courts, where the inmates play *pelota paleta*. All these trees are making me dizzy, I need a rest.

I buy cigarettes at the kiosk next to the office, I smoke and feel calmer. Jaime must be about to come by to look for me, he said two o' clock. Despite being a rural type, he's quite punctual.

Suddenly I get the feeling that someone is speaking to me, it must be him. No, it's the man with the sunglasses and Coke. Yes, now I recognise him, but it makes no sense. It's Yasky, the court clerk, in flesh and blood, a mere five metres from where I'm standing, masked by those old-fashioned motorcycle sunglasses, too bulky for the size of his face, which make him look ridiculous, a cross between a fly and a premature baby. Without his suit, he's unrecognisable. But what's he doing here? Why didn't he summons me if he wanted to see me? I don't understand. The first thing that springs to mind is that there must be some outstanding legal matter, that I didn't tell the whole truth and a single word clouds my eyes: perjury. Then my memory clears, of giving the statement in the police station, the pitted face of the obese, gum-chewing officer who spoke into his walkie-talkie as he typed at the computer, and my statement at the court with Yasky's legs kicking me under the desk, and me, I SWEAR, in capital letters, and I sign at the bottom, here, and here as well, and it's true, I confess, I did keep some things to myself, things that, well, by now I don't even know how they really happened. I'll tell him anything he wants, but he doesn't give me time. He approaches. Yasky stops half a metre away, takes off his sunglasses and holds out his sweaty hand, which I take in mine. I'm trembling, noticeably. What a surprise, I manage to say. And him: yes, what a coincidence. He's shaking even more than I am. It doesn't look like he's here to arrest me. I'm not in front of Yasky the court clerk, it's something else, I can see it in his eyes, slightly watery and shrunken, which barely look at me, only as long as they have to, then immediately they dart away, looking at the sky, the ground, an emergency exit, any which way. I calm down. I'm living nearby, behind the hospital, I say gesturing vaguely at somewhere far away. Yes, of course, he says. He talks and every so often he glances to either side, searching. And the business with Aída, no news? I ask quickly, to take the weight off my shoulders. Yasky seems lost, he's not listening, he's looking around. My friend, the one from the bridge. Yes, a very unusual case, the coastguard aren't getting anywhere, or even worse, they find . . . the thing the other day, for example . . . and he doesn't finish the sentence because this time his searching eyes find something: two loonies. One with long hair, regulation blue shirt and trousers, barefoot. The other, in a white t-shirt with a photo of a sailing boat on the front, is, paler and unkempt, a carbon copy of Yasky: the same round face, the classic bearing, the short neck, hairy, neither fat nor thin, a lunatic version of Yasky. They approach and stop a few metres away, taking me in from a distance, heads bowed.

'This is Julio, my brother,' says Yasky and widens his eyes for me to say my name.

Now Julio speaks, talking to his brother.

'This is Omar . . . I told him to come along so you could meet him . . . no, he won't speak to you, he understands but he doesn't speak, I told him you were here and that we should come and see you . . . can we have another Coke?'

Omar is somewhere else, he's inoffensive. He blinks

more than is normal, and when his eyes close, he tries to fight it.

The four of us sit down, Yasky, the two loonies and I, around a small white garden table.

'I'm fine,' says Julio, 'I'm fine . . . how do you think I look? . . . when the telly's not working I get a bit bored . . . just now it's working . . . can we go for a drive in the car? I told Omar you'd lend us the car for a little drive . . . without leaving the grounds, just a little while, he understands everything, can we?'

Yasky doesn't reply and Julio doesn't complain. It's as though they've had this conversation before. A code between brothers.

I tell Yasky that Jaime, my friend (I don't know what to call him: boyfriend, lover, carer, country boy, could he be my country boy?) works in the hospital's plant nursery. But Yasky doesn't want to hear about anything to do with the hospital and immediately changes the subject.

'It's a mystery, it makes no sense, even with a strong current or at high tide, that stretch is narrow and not very deep, a body can't disappear just like that.'

'There are vipers,' says Omar, the one who doesn't speak, and we all fall silent.

After a while, Jaime appeared in the pick-up and beeped the horn, so I said my goodbyes quickly. Yasky stood up and didn't know whether to hold out his hand or risk a kiss on the cheek. It turned out to be neither, something between the two, and he ended up having to manage a balancing act, almost falling.

'Well, it was a pleasure,' he said. And a second later, as I was walking away, he almost shouts:

'I'm Bernardo.'

There is a small path leading from the stable, almost overgrown with bushes, skirting the mill, then getting lost behind a hillock. A tight, zigzagging path.

I start walking along it. It's quite a nice afternoon, with an autumn sun coming and going, appearing and hiding at intervals. An unstable sun. Past the hillock, the path turns to the right and leads to a ring of trees, of medium height but quite dense. I'm not sure, but it strikes me that they could be the olive trees that Jaime mentioned once.

Now that I'm up close, what I thought was there isn't there, the ring isn't such a ring, and the trees aren't that dense. From a distance, the colours of the countryside are hard to distinguish, they bind together. The sunshine doesn't help. What had seemed to be a small oasis rising up from the middle of the plain turns out to be a cluster of old trunks, dry, pointed branches that devastate everything, a sort of giant crown of thorns for a super-Christ. I bend down and as I slip through to the far side of the fence I catch my neck. Ouch.

On this side of the fence there is an Australian-style water tank, a couple of metres tall, so completely abandoned that it can't have been filled for several summers now. The metal sheeting was painted once upon a time, but I can't tell whether it's meant to be blue or green. I stand on my toes to peek over the edge, but I can't, it's higher than I thought.

I walk around it and come to some tiny aluminium steps attached to the side of the tank. The first thing I see is a layer of oddly coloured gelatinous filth, a nameless mixture of many browns verging on black. And although there is no particular odour, that non-colour floating at the bottom smells horrible.

But there's more. Amongst the dry leaves, the fallen branches and the slimy algae, in that sub-world containing the worst of plant life, a kite is sticking out. The wreck of a kite, almost unrecognisable. It's a deliberate image, a visual effect: a dead kite. A cliché. I don't know why I feel so sad all of a sudden. Like I haven't felt for a long time. So sad that I let myself slump to the ground, I close my eyes and I touch myself, I stroke myself, for consolation. And that's how I spend the afternoon.

NINETEEN

I make mistakes: I act too hastily, on impulse, like a child.

Jaime was going to the village to send a fax to the ministry to initiate his retirement process. I'll go with you, I said, and that made him happy. I got into the truck and started the engine while Jaime finished getting some papers together. I turned on the radio and the only thing I could pick up properly was the exultant voice of an evangelical pastor talking in a strange mix of Spanish and Portuguese. Every two or three phrases, a euphoric crowd celebrated his sermon with hoarse cries that lengthened the *o* of glory into paroxysm. It could have been recorded or live, it could have been a joke or serious, it didn't matter.

I was about to switch off the radio but I waited for a second to see Jaime's reaction. But Jaime didn't react, and I tired first. We went past the door of the shop, it looked closed. To tell the truth, it always looks closed. We passed a man wearing a military-green beret who was cycling in the opposite direction. Jaime sounded the horn unwillingly and it produced a toneless electric noise, like a death rattle. The man in the beret raised an arm in greeting and almost lost his balance. Jaime looked at me as though he wanted to tell me who it was, or for me to ask him: Who's that? I didn't give him the pleasure.

We stopped at the service station to fill up with diesel. Jaime greeted everyone again, as usual. I got out to buy some gum at the kiosk. Two guys wearing the company uniform, waiting on tiny benches for their turn to serve the next client, were giving me sidelong glances. They weren't watching me: they were keeping me under surveillance. It was the best remedy for boredom in this circular village, which already knew everything about me and what it didn't, it invented. Before we left, through some half-paranoid instinct, which sooner or later makes us utterly paranoid, I turned my head, just slightly, just for a second, just long enough to see how the third man, the one who had exchanged a few words with Jaime as he watched the numbers run up on the pump, approached the other two, adding his conspiratorial laugh, loaded with innuendo that secretly named me.

For the rest of the journey to the shopping centre, Jaime stayed silent. A silence that I almost filled with words that I chewed over in my head several times and then aborted without ever opening my mouth.

'I don't know how long I'll be, I have to send the fax, then get that man, the what d'you call him, the administrator, to confirm that it arrived safely. Why don't you take a walk?'

Jaime had stepped out of the pick-up and was speaking with his hand on the door. Since I don't reply, not out of meanness but because I don't know what I want, he gives me the keys so that I can feel free.

'Here,' he says, 'if you go, lock up, I'll be over here.'

In giving me the keys, Jaime behaves as a father would, and I'm like a teenage daughter. So, to follow to the letter the logic of this bad-tempered girl I've become, as soon as he can no longer see me, I get out of the pick-up and start strolling, as he suggested, but without his knowing.

It's half twelve, the daylight is as hazy as it was a few hours ago and it's going to stay like this until it gets dark. It's the middle of autumn, any old day, forgettable. I leave the shopping centre behind me and wander along an unpaved street at right angles to the main avenue, with my back to the school building. Most of the trees are already bare and the privet hedges forming the boundaries between houses are quite stunted. I'm distracted by noises that come from close by or far away, some continuous and subtle, like the humming of an insect that doesn't let itself be seen, others more violent, appearing suddenly and cutting out just as abruptly. I'm never going to get used to country noises. There aren't many of them, and yet they are so precise. They always reveal something. And hide the rest.

Right at that moment, as I was beginning to get bored of the empty village streets, a different, complex sound surprises me, one that I wasn't expecting to hear. There are several voices, all talking at once, rapidly, on top of one another, in rather high-pitched tones. Voices that sound very near but which don't show their faces. There isn't a soul to either side, no one behind, no one up ahead, and yet they're so close. I walk on a couple of metres, focused on the murmuring, which is growing in intensity. I even manage to trap a few words in the air, like 'evening', 'wearing', 'damn', 'Friday', and I'm the closest thing to a lunatic who hears voices. The madness doesn't last long. I don't even have time to react: in less than a second I become a mess of nerves. Some four or five girls, all in the same school uniform, white blouse and kilt, come out of the garage of the house on the corner, five metres from where I'm standing. And the first thing I see, as if there were nothing else, before I see the uniforms, the garage, is Eloísa, so wrapped up in the conversation that she doesn't register I'm here, so close, by pure coincidence. It's best she doesn't see me, I'd better turn round, without a sound. Yes, that's the best way.

But anxiety gets the better of me and I follow a narrow dirt alley so that I can go round and meet her at the cross-roads. I have to be surprised, it has to be natural, as if by chance.

There's no one in the other street. Not a voice or a sound to be heard. The house from which Eloísa and the other girls came has an entrance on this street too, at the end. I don't understand. I take a new street, then another, and I'm lost.

I turn on my heel and find myself on the first street again. From there I go out onto the main avenue, I'm three blocks from the shopping centre. I bend down to tie my shoelace and without warning, the girls appear. Eloísa's at the front, I smile at her, but she keeps going. She completely ignores me. I catch a flying sentence suspended in the air as they move away.

'She's such a maggot,' says one them who isn't Eloísa. I wonder who they're talking about. I stare after the little group, which forms a kind of arrow with Eloísa at the tip. I don't know whether to follow them, I don't know whether to join in, I don't know what to do. At the corner, before turning, Eloísa looks back and waves her hand, laughing from a distance. I feel stupid.

I return to the shopping centre without lifting my eyes from the ground, like a fool, feeling put out. Jaime is waiting for me at the foot of the pick-up, the keys in his hand.

'You left the keys in the ignition,' he says and adds with an unbearable smile: 'It's not a good idea.'

I don't answer, grabbing the keys from him and getting into the truck. I switch on the radio. I'm beginning to tire of his moroseness, his persistent nothingness. Jaime looks up at me, his hands now busy with tobacco and rolling papers. He looks at me, intrigued, with the subtle estrangement that used to make him that bit different. He watches me with the expression of an old man who's seen it all before.

The next day, by the bare fig tree, Eloísa strokes my hair:

'See over there?'

'Where?'

'There, between the shop and the mill.'

'What is it?'

'That ranch, see? Some gypsies are occupying it.'

'And who does it belong to?'

'Nobody. They say that they're Romanians. I don't know how they ended up here.'

'Who can have tipped them off about it?' I say, and the question floats in the air.

TWENTY

Jaime brought home a television. He must see that I'm bored. He spent all afternoon trying to install the antenna. All we see is roughly equally spaced lines on every channel. The only thing that is occasionally clear is the sound. We hear parts of dialogues, distorted adverts, distant presenters. He eventually gave in, returned the set to its box and put it in the stable, rather embarrassed.

On Tuesday morning I returned to the library to pick up my translation. I opened the door but Brenda wasn't in her usual place. She couldn't have been far away, however, because there were a couple of books open on the desk, in use: a Spanish-Latin dictionary, a volume of an encyclopaedia and a writing pad with fresh notes on it. I went into the reading room, but there was no one there either. I said hello twice and even called her name.

'Brenda,' I threw the word into the air, in no particular

direction, but Brenda didn't appear.

Now that I looked closely, in the far corner of the room, in a straight line with the desk, there was a small door slightly ajar, camouflaged against the wall. I knocked gently and the door opened by itself. It led to a back patio covered with a dry vine. An iron table with four matching chairs stood in the centre of the patio. Further on there were two more doors. I went forward a few metres. One of the doors led to a spacious kitchen, the other to a bedroom with two identical beds, perfectly made, each watched over by a crucifix on the headboard. Without meaning to, surreptitiously, I had entered Brenda's house, I had looked into its privacy. Curiosity grabbed me: Which came first, the house or the library? What had been turned into what?

As I wondered about that, standing in the middle of the patio, I almost fell when a sharp cry returned me to reality in the cruellest way. I leant on the back of one of the chairs, which I now realised wasn't made of iron like the others but was the wheelchair that Brenda used to get about. I looked all around me until I saw a fourth door, made of tin, halfway between the house and the library.

'Brenda, are you there?' I said, this time almost whispering, with a certain amount of fear.

The door opened in slow motion, creaking every millimetre of the way until finally I could see Brenda sitting on the toilet with her knickers down, her face covered in drops of sweat or tears, I don't know which. But what caught my eye the most were her ears, the lobes slashed with fine cuts, recently made.

With gestures, Brenda asked me to bring over her chair and help her to change seats. Of course I didn't inquire about any of the strange things I'd just observed, nor did it occur to me to question the unusual distance between her wheelchair and the bathroom door. Could someone have played a trick on her, or had the chair simply rolled towards the others?

When Brenda had regained her composure and taken her place behind the desk once more, all I managed to ask her was whether she was all right. In fact, I was about to leave without mentioning the translation, it didn't seem the best time for it. But my silence was seemingly eloquent because Brenda immediately opened a drawer, handed me the book by Huret and tore five or six leaves, neatly handwritten in black pencil, from the pad.

'It's the best I could do,' she said in a slightly hoarse voice. I left without saying anything, full of doubts.

On the way back to the farm, my thoughts occupied with Brenda's wounded ears, I took a rest and skimmed the first few paragraphs of the translation:

A model establishment, of which very few still exist in Europe, operates in Luján, one hour away from Buenos Aires, in the middle of the flourishing countryside. Founded by the State, on the whim of an extraordinary man, blessed with a pleasant and smiling vitality, to whom it is impossible to deny anything, this work is wholly prosperous and produces surprising results.

Dr Cabred is the driving force behind this movement. President of the national hospitals commission, he promotes, with his vigorous activity and contagious enthusiasm, the creation of modern colonies for the insane throughout the Republic. He knows France and Paris perfectly, as he does the hospitals in which he studied under the guidance of our masters. But the models for his establishment he took from Scotland and Germany, where the 'open door' system has been successfully practised for many years, as it has in Russia and the United States. He was particularly inspired, in respect of the plans and details of the facility, by the Alt-Scherbitz asylum, near Dresden in Saxony. The open door method is not yet widely applied in France, where progress is slow. Dr Cabred is extremely passionate. He claims that lunatics are made furious by precisely the coercion that is exercised on their liberty, the liberty to come and go, to move about.

'Now there are no furious lunatics, except in cases of acute crisis,' Dr Cabred explains to me. 'It is the old method of treatment that made them mad. Instead of being on top of each other, getting worked up, over-excited, here they are free to come and go, to be alone, to work, to walk about; they don't think about escaping (we have only one breakout per hundred patients), nor rebelling, nor shouting, nor fighting: they are free!'

TWENTY-ONE

At first Boca's shouts are in my dream, but they don't say anything, nor do they belong to Boca. They are deformed shouts, filled with fury, the cries of someone running out of air and on the point of suffocating. The voice becomes flesh, too close. Boca shouts as hard as his throat will allow, from the other side of the wall: Fire, fire, fire. Jaime gives a start, elbowing me in the stomach. I half open my eyes. Boca's shadow is moving like a madman from one side of the veranda to the other and he howls fire three times again. Jaime gets up as best he can without switching on the light and heads for the kitchen. I'm trembling. Without moving from the bed, in the dark, I hear the sound of the bolt being drawn back and the door opening. A long silence follows, Boca's face must say it all. Jaime comes back into the room, sits on the edge of the bed and hesitates for a few seconds before putting on his trousers and boots, just in case someone comes to tell him not to bother, to lie down again, that it's not true. He speaks in the dark, in a low voice so as not to wake me:

'He says the stable's on fire.'

Eloísa came to see me with a bunch of gigantic hydrangeas and a discoloured rose, a wild bouquet, gathered on her way.

'I picked them for you,' she says. 'Do you like them? Let's put them in some water.'

We have lunch together, without Jaime, and we stay in the kitchen playing cards for a long time.

Later it began to rain and we had to close the shutters because water was coming in all over the place. At the kitchen table, clutching a maté gourd, Eloísa doesn't stop talking, she tells me everything. Is this your room, she asks and by the time I catch up with her she's already going through the wardrobe. I sit on the edge of the bed, while Eloísa takes down as many hangers as she can hold and embraces my few clothes, which are mixed up with a suede bag belonging to Jaime. She examines them, enthusing over some, criticising others, making a thousand gestures with her eyebrows and lips, until she chooses one, letting the rest fall to the floor.

'Can I try it on?'

I smile. Eloísa undresses. She wants to impress me.

TWENTY-TWO

It must be the coldest day of the year, everyone has a scarf tied round their neck. Some are wearing hats, even gloves. The morgue looks different in the winter, it becomes less drastic. This is the third time I've been here in less than three months. I hope this will be the end of it. Yasky summonsed me at short notice because Monday is a bank holiday, which complicates everything as far as the police are concerned, he explained on the phone. Jaime wanted to give me a lift, but a small job came up, so he said, at the last minute.

The procedure is quicker than usual because the administration office has already closed for the weekend, which speeds up the bureaucracy. I had come mentally prepared to continue the game with the ginger man and to see how far it would go but it will have to wait for next time, although perhaps there won't be a next time, yeah, I hope not.

The man on duty uncovers the body and I can't help spitting out a laugh which is more like a sneeze: the corpse has a beard and a moustache. Yasky releases a shout that disconcerts the poor man.

'What is this?' says Yasky in a voice louder than I thought him capable. The man hurries to cover the body and Yasky grabs him by the arm, leading him out of the room. They leave me alone with a collection of corpses, which must be signalling to me in silence. I'm not needed here, I leave before one of them decides to talk to me.

Coffee in hand, standing by the counter in a student bar where a radio is blaring rock music at full blast, Yasky attempts to explain the inexplicable.

'There was a mix-up,' he says biting the rim of the plastic cup, between sips of coffee. 'Someone put a cross in the wrong place, they marked *f* instead of *m*, it's outrageous. I don't understand how no one realised. The weekend comes around and their heads are all over the place. I've never seen anything like it in my entire career, I'm going to open an investigation first thing on Tuesday. I don't know what to tell you.'

I tell him not to worry about me, that all this business has made me immune. Yasky relaxes, his mood changes and he asks me if I wouldn't like to go for a drink in another bar, somewhere less noisy. He asks me in the negative, as many men do. OK, I say, let's go. On the way there it hits me: Yasky wanted me to come just to be able to see me again. He fancies me, or worse, he's fallen in love with me. He summonsed me because that way I couldn't refuse to come, I'm duty bound, and because this is our place, the place where we meet. I humour him.

In the second bar, we sit at a table at the back and order a beer. After exchanging a few comments about this winter, which arrived without warning, overnight, Yasky leaves a long pause, takes a slug of beer, tipping up his pint until it's empty, and starts speaking about his brother Julio. He talks as though he owes me an explanation about that as well. His eyes are glistening.

'Sometimes I think that it could just as easily have been me, these things don't depend on the individual, it's pure chance. I've often wondered what the reasons were, whether there was a trigger, some episode that I missed, but it doesn't change anything, I always just end up tying myself in knots. And don't forget that Julio and I are the same age.'

'Yes,' I say, 'you look like twins.'

'Not just twins, we're identical twins, but it makes no difference, we go through the same things.'

With Yasky, time passes very slowly. Even so, night falls and I don't want to return to the countryside. I'm scared of running into Eloísa.

'It's late' says Yasky. 'Can I take you anywhere?'

'Is your place far?' is the first thing to come out of my mouth and Yasky is eager.

It's a two-room flat, facing away from the street, decorated without enthusiasm, a pastiche of furniture and tasteless objects, lots of glass and lots of wicker. Yasky asks me where I want to sleep. It's your house, I say.

'My room's a disaster, I'd better not even show it to you. A bachelor pad,' he says, and laughs. We laugh. In the living room, there's a polka-dot sofa-bed. Yasky unfolds it and starts to extol its virtues: the cushions are built in, the mattress is queen-size, more comfortable than a lot of beds. It's as though he wants to sell it to me. I wonder when he's going to jump on me.

Next to the head of the sofa-bed there's a black telephone with keys that light up when I unhook the receiver. I call Jaime and tell him that I'm staying in Buenos Aires, at a girlfriend's house.

'It got late, I'll be back early tomorrow.'

'And the girl? Was it her?'

I stay mute, as does Jaime. He murmurs a sad goodbye before hanging up.

Yasky brings out some blue sheets patterned with shooting stars and apologises for them:

'I've still got them from when I was a teenager.'

And although he says it in reference to the sheets, Yasky is talking about himself, he's confessing, behind the court clerk there's a teenager with problems. He goes into the bathroom, leaving me alone, I don't know what I'm doing here.

I grab the phone again and dial rapidly, without thinking. Eloísa answers, half asleep. I hang up. It might have been her mum, the doubt lingers.

Later, with coffee, the chat flows again, we talk about everything. To tell the truth, he talks, jumping from topic to topic without pause. He's happy. He tells me about university, about everything he gave up to live for his studies, he mentions Esteban a hundred times, the best friend he's known since primary school and who he sees every Thursday night, come what may. He lights up when he talks about his father, who died two years ago and left him this little flat, which isn't the house he would have chosen to live in, but which isn't bad, it's enough for him on his own, and the location is unbeatable, everything's on the doorstep.

My eyes close, Yasky resists, he still has one topic left, his passion for the racetrack. He loves it, he doesn't miss a single Sunday.

'But I control myself,' he cuts himself short. 'I'm far from an addict.'

Finally he shuts up and I make the most of the pause to shut him up completely.

'Bernardo,' I say in a low voice, as if to keep it between the two of us. 'I'm a virgin.'

His face freezes, he doesn't get the joke. I seem to have offended him. Yasky arches his eyebrows in a sign of annoyance and starts washing the dishes, charging the atmosphere with a melodramatic silence. He must feel ridiculous because in a minute he gets over it and suggests we see if there are any films on. With the television on, we forget about everything. Me, about Aída, who still hasn't shown up, and about Eloísa's hands exploring my body, and life in the country which is starting to drive me insane, and that story about lunatics from a century ago, which intrigues me, I still don't know why. Yasky must be trying to erase my joke from his mind, which I'm sure will torture him all night.

At about one o'clock, the blank screen barking the apocalyptic noise that marks the end of transmission, we go to sleep in separate rooms, like an old-fashioned marriage.

TWENTY-THREE

The Romanians on the ranch have a party every night. They start early, at around half eight, sometimes a bit earlier to prepare the bonfire. Eloísa and I smoke in the storeroom behind the shop, about a hundred metres from where they are. Without meaning to, we fall silent to listen to them, to see what they're doing. They talk loudly, they sing, they play the guitar, and as the hours slip by some of them become violent, they break bottles, insult each other, or rather they shout things that sound like insults. They almost go insane.

Eloísa tells me that one of the Romanians goes to the shop to buy flour and gin. She says he has a kind face and he's handsome, if a bit dirty. She asked him his name but as she didn't understand his reply, he wrote it on a piece of card. Eloísa shows it to me. I read: Loti. Eloísa laughs.

'Isn't it a ridiculous name?'

•

Iosi Havilio

Inside the Huret book, folded into four, I found a piece of yellowed paper, stained by time, and written on a typewriter with annotations in the margins.

> *Inebriation and insanity. By Domingo Faustino Sarmiento. Reading at a meeting of doctors in his house on July 29th, 1884.*
>
> *Conclusions:*
> *1st – As far as the production or cause of dementia is concerned, the statistics from the dementia hospices are inevitably incomplete.*
> *2nd – The dementia of today is the peculiar condition of an imperfect civilisation.*
> *3rd – The alien population in America vastly increases the number of elements, and acts indirectly as an element, of generation or production of dementia in the native population.*
> *4th – Heredity, whether in relation to physical, intellectual or moral conditions, is of greater importance in the production of dementia than generally supposed.*
> *5th – Poor education, lack of it, or superficial education, increases the number of demented individuals, while on the other hand, a good system of moral and scholarly education has great influence in the prevention of dementia.*
> *6th – Certain occupations are more conducive than others to the development of dementia, whilst lack of occupation is frequently a cause, and on occasion a symptom, of dementias.*
> *7th – Unhealthy marriages increase dementia, and single men, and probably single women too, are more prone to*

dementia than married couples. Furthermore, marriages between blood relatives are shown, with much uncertainty and in very rare cases, to be the exception to this.

Yesterday one of them committed suicide, Jaime tells me at breakfast, as Boca swings the axe on the other side of the window and Martín piles the wood against the wall of the veranda.

TWENTY-FOUR

Jaime had gone out on a job with Boca. They had to change the roof tiles of a ranch house on an estate about two hundred kilometres from Open Door. We're going to spend a few nights there, until we finish the job, said Jaime and asked me whether I was scared to be left alone. Not at all.

An hour after Jaime left, Eloísa appeared, in perfect synchrony, as if she had planned it. She brought a generous fistful of hash that she could barely contain in her hand. There's enough here to smoke five a day for a week, she said, placing the small mountain of marijuana in a bowl on top of the fridge. It was three in the afternoon, we had to pass the time somehow. Let's have a bath together, suggested Eloísa. It seemed like a good idea, so I prepared the tub for the two of us while Eloísa rolled the first joint, leaving another ready for later.

I snogged the Romanian in the storeroom, Eloísa tells me casually as she undresses. He's a sweetie, a really good kisser, she says. Did I tell you that he's called Loti? Isn't it funny? Loti, Loti, Loti, she repeats, as if it were a game. I still have no idea how old she is: it's all the same to me, but it's strange, sometimes I put her at seventeen, sometimes thirty-five. Eloísa continues to tell me about Loti, gently pinching my bum between sentences. Did you know he's got a gold tooth?

We spend the whole afternoon in the water, without kissing or anything. Eloísa taught me some new songs by a rock group she's fanatical about. She sings badly, but I like it. We smoked the joint, and half of the second one, which slipped from my fingers and fell into the water. We laughed a lot, about Jaime, about Boca, about the poseurs who play polo, about the shape of my feet, rather crooked and crablike, and about a load of other nonsense.

I don't know why it occurred to me to tell her about Aída. To fill a gap, or because I sobered up and it seemed a good moment to confess. Eloísa became serious when I mentioned the bridge. Her seriousness lasted about as long as the fall did, less than a minute. And with her smoke-filled cackles, feeling rather dizzy, I suddenly understood everything: the precision of chance, the cosmic, the inevitable.

The night caught us dozing, still naked, brushing against each other time and again, in Jaime's bed.

Eloísa lit another joint, our third, and a ferocious hunger attacked us, which we sated by emptying the larder of anything edible: noodles, tuna, breadcrumbs, *turrón* and birdseed. Then we went back to bed.

'Do you want me to go down on you?' asks Eloísa out of nowhere, once we've switched off the light.

•

Jaime came in slowly, noiselessly, in the middle of the night. His head appeared first, he was almost on tiptoe. Eloísa was curled up between my legs, under the blanket, barely visible. She was breathing hard, her nose blocked with mucus. Jaime came in slowly, noiselessly, but I saw him out of the corner of my eye. He stayed on the threshold without letting go of the handle, leaning on it, then he disappeared.

I put on the first thing I could find, a long jumper with buttons, a kind of cardigan. I lit a cigarette and went into the kitchen in bare feet, shivering. Jaime had his back to me, trying to hurry the kettle to a boil. I grabbed a chair and dragged it back needlessly, to attract his attention, but Jaime didn't turn round. I spoke first.

'You're back early.'

'They brought me back,' he says, 'the truck broke down on the way.'

'And how did it go?'

'It was a fiasco,' he says and turns round, with the same expression as always, a bit paler than usual with a nervous laugh biting his lips. He doesn't look at me, he talks to the kettle which is now steaming.

'That guy is a swindler,' he says and I can't help laughing.

'A swindler,' I repeat quietly, 'that's funny.'

'Not to me,' grumbles Jaime, 'he makes me drive 200 kilometres on a fool's errand and to crown it all we're left stranded in the middle of the road.'

Jaime's language is old-fashioned, provincial, sometimes I forget that he's a country boy and that, by now, I must be a country boy's girl. A new generation of country girls.

'And the kid . . . ?' he finally brings himself to ask, gesturing towards the bedroom with his chin.

'It's Eloísa, the girl from the shop.'

'Yes, I know.'

'We were chatting until late, and I told her she could stay here, she's just a kid.' I don't know why I add the last part, it wasn't necessary. Jaime lifts his chin once more to indicate the bedroom as if to say: Oh right, or well, well, or even: Is the girl going to be in my bed for long? When he's lost for words, Jaime points with his chin to complete his sentence, as if he's neighing.

Grudgingly, Jaime says we'll wait until morning, there's no point in waking her and making her leave at this time of night. Not entirely convinced, he goes and slumps in the armchair next to the chimney. Eloísa is sitting on the bed waiting for me, in a Buddha position.

'Get dressed and go, Jaime's back, he's in the next room,' I say and she throws herself on top of me, tickling me. Leave, I tell her, and half joking, half serious, I give her a kick which knocks her out of bed. And, from the floor, naked, unabashed, she laughs like a loony. She opens her legs and shows me everything. She mocks: Get dressed and go, imitating my voice and she throws herself on top of me again. She sits on my back and grips my wrists as if she has the strength to pin me down. I let her defeat me although I say, just for the sake of it: OK, Eloísa, that's enough. And she repeats in a commanding voice, the most serious she can summon: OK,

Eloísa, that's enough. Now she lets me go and gets back under the sheets, she quietens down. Then I turn over and grab her head so hard that I surprise myself and bury it between my legs. She freezes slightly, I guide her, I teach her. She learns quickly, and she practises, for the rest of the night, until it gets light. Do you like it? she asks quietly, and I grit my teeth. Jaime doesn't show his face again, or at least I don't see him.

Eloísa stays for breakfast. We drink mugs of maté and eat bread with butter and sugar.

'I like horses too, we had one until recently, it was half mine and half my brother's. We called it Tato, after a mad uncle who lives in Misiones, but my old man sold it to pay off some debts at the shop,' says Eloísa and Jaime looks at her as though he wants her far away.

Come with me to the gate, Eloísa asks in my ear. Once we are a reasonable distance from the house, she grabs my hand, trying to interlace her fingers with mine, she says nothing, nor do I, there's no need. Before going through the gate, she kisses me quickly on the lips.

'I had a great time, thank you,' she says, and I can't quite believe she said thank you.

Jaime and Boca spend all day fixing the pick-up, one underneath, between the wheels, the other with his head buried in the engine. I tend to the house, I sweep, I cook, I make the bed, like an automaton. To get Eloísa out of my head, I lie down in a deck chair with Brenda's pages and start reading at random, without paying too much attention, as if praying.

'*Open Door is built in the middle of the Luján plain, not far from a famous cathedral, the best-known pilgrimage site in Argentina. The establishment is divided into two distinct parts: on one side, the central asylum, which holds the administrative and hospital services, and houses for patients under full-time surveillance or in temporary isolation; on the other side, the open door and agricultural work colony.*

'*No walls restrict the horizon, nothing to limit the illusion of absolute liberty. The establishment is composed of fourteen separate blocks, rooms, workshops, kitchens and offices, whose white facades and red roofs are scattered happily through the green countryside. The interior is just as cheerful as the exterior: corridors and verandas with white walls, floor tiles of different colours and flowers at the windows. From the open blocks comes the sound of songs and gramophone orchestras. It is hard to imagine a working establishment more perfect than this.*'

'That's it sorted, it was the carburettor,' says Jaime, coming into the kitchen, and adds: 'I don't want you to see that girl anymore, the one from the shop. That kind of girl brings trouble.'

Later that same day, Eloísa asks me whether I've tried ket. Ketamine, she says and I laugh. We laugh. We're sitting on the bank of the stream, her behind me, scratching my back underneath my blouse. Have you never tried it? Not even out of curiosity? My friends, she says, take it when they go dancing.

TWENTY-FIVE

Curled up by the chimney, I pass the time hypnotised by the fire, spellbound. My eyes follow the path of the flames. It's crazy, the way everything changes, so quickly, so imperceptibly. And by the time I've registered it, there it is, it's already changed. There are those first timid flames that need to be revived by blowing, then the powerful ones that wrap around trunks and branches, from the smallest to the largest, the thinnest to the thickest. Each flame follows its own path. Sometimes, for some reason that escapes me, the fire swirls and forms corkscrews that come and go from yellow to red, so frenziedly. And they hollow out the wood, forming eyes in it. But from a distance, the most fascinating, beautiful, and at the same time terrible part is the moment of destruction. The burning wood splitting into two, falling into pieces, turning into smoke. They are tiny catastrophes, homemade, controlled, miniature cataclysms. Jaime is standing in silence behind me. He's watching too.

Away from the fire and its charms, the truth is that it's brutally cold and if we don't move away from the chimney it's because we can't bear to be in the rest of the house. The kitchen is freezing and we can't even bring ourselves to enter the bedroom, it's almost certainly worse.

'A rat,' Jaime says suddenly, his voice changed, rather hoarse, so much so that I have to turn round because I'm not sure I've heard correctly.

'What?'

'A rat,' he repeated, slightly irritated and, despite not having seen anything resembling a rat, I climb onto a chair, just in case, it seems like the obvious thing to do. Jaime took a shotgun off the wall and pointed it downwards, in every direction, towards the armchair, the door, the chimney, always downwards. I took a moment to react, mainly because I could have sworn that the gun was purely decorative. Jaime continued with his hunt, his face red and overwhelmed. I still hadn't worked out whether this was a joke or not. To further confuse me, Jaime talked to it, to the rat, about all sorts of things. He talked to it more than he'd spoken to me all day. He was saying: Come out, you bastard, come out of there, you lousy bastard, and he stamped and kicked the furniture, he tried to make it move but the rat didn't reveal itself. Jaime kept going for some time, so long that I began to get bored perching on the chair, and I sat down and started watching the fire again. At one point, I looked behind me and my eyes met Jaime's as if to ask him: Are you sure you saw a rat? But he averted his gaze immediately, he was engrossed in this opponentless duel, his gun still pointing at the floor, although carelessly now, without precision.

All this time, the fire had made and unmade a thousand things. It was impossible to reconstruct the path of the flames. Of some thin branches that I remembered from before, nothing remained but confused traces with no identity. They had become embers, and the embers ashes. The fire, which by now was looking a bit lifeless, needed to be fed. Order needed to be imposed to restore the calm.

I was getting up to do just that when a strange, living weight, from another world, dropped onto my right shoulder and looked me in the eye. And now there was no doubt. There it was, clinging to my body like a fairground parrot, a country rat in flesh and blood. And it was so different from the picture I'd had in my mind, so big and solid, it was anything but a rat. But how had it landed on my shoulder? I'll never know. The truth is that it was on me for a very short time, a fraction of a second, which at that moment seemed like a year and a half. Just long enough to look me in the eye, then it jumped.

Jaime let out a gruff shout, like a caveman. He threw a half brick, I don't know where he got it, and when he thought he'd cornered the beast, he began to shoot, point-blank, like a madman. He shot, reloaded, shot, reloaded again and shot, I lost count how many times. I closed my eyes, on reflex, and like that, with my eyes tight shut, it felt just like being caught up in a shootout in a film. Blindly, I had gone into the kitchen, either instinctively or because Jaime had pushed me there, I can't remember. I sat down, opened my eyes carefully and observed the scene with my mouth half open and my fists clenched close to my neck to support my head. I watched what I could, what the angle and frame of the door would allow me to see. Finally the last shot rang out, followed by that humming stillness that comes after the firing subsides.

I peeked out. The armchair was destroyed and near the chimney there is still a hole today, about the size of a grapefruit, the source of which no one will ever guess. Jaime poked through what remained of the chair with the tip of the gun and discovered the decapitated rat in a corner. He was dripping sweat and I wasn't sure that he hadn't been crying a bit too.

Embarrassed, Jaime went to the kitchen to get a shovel without looking at me. He scooped up the animal, covered it with rubble and went out of the house with the shovel in his hand. He took it far away. And he stayed outside, he must have been thinking or smoking, because it took him half an hour to return.

I went back to the fireside and managed to revive the flames just before they went out. It was going to be a long night.

TWENTY-SIX

In the same way that Boca's gruff shouts a few days ago had woken us to the fire devouring half the stable, not so much a loss for Jaime as a way to bury the horse for good, Eloísa was dragging us from our sleep by clapping her hands on the veranda. This time it was during siesta, a longer siesta than usual.

Jaime had brought out a box full of photos, which we had begun to look through as we lay on the bed. Old photos, almost sepia, from when the two Jaimes were young. At the racetrack, in the colony, at the stable door, by the side of the road. Jaime was a young man, not yet forty, with a moustache and ridiculous sideburns, his hair slicked back tightly with gel or pomade. He had an intense gaze, proud and macho. We came across a blurred photo of Jaime and a very pale woman with a kind face, raising their glasses in a restaurant with hams hanging down from the ceiling. Jaime and his wife, the wife he never mentions. He held the photo between his fingers for three long seconds without speaking. Perhaps he was waiting for me to ask about her, but the truth is I didn't particularly want to find out. He kept passing me photos, in colour or black and white, every single one he had, photos of men posing with their arms around each other, Jaime in the middle, the countryside always there in the background. Afterwards, before he did, I fell asleep.

Eloísa clapped again and the echo of her hands colliding made the sheets vibrate. It was quarter to eight. Jaime stretched towards the window without getting out of bed, raised the blinds, and was met by Eloísa's face in close-up at the window. A slightly out-of-focus Eloísa, seen through the mosquito net, tinted yellow by the light of the veranda. Poor Jaime, silently exasperated, flopped back onto the mattress.

'It's for you,' he said, after a very theatrical pause.

I was always touched by the way that Eloísa, in spite of everything, in spite of herself, maintained certain customs of the countryside, such as clapping to announce her presence when she arrived at someone's house. The thing is that Eloísa, deep down, was a simple country girl, and sometimes she forgot that.

I went into the kitchen, switched on the light, pushed open the door with my naked toes and felt the damp bricks of the veranda cold against my soles. Barely visible, standing with her back to me at the edge of the shaft of light, Eloísa lit a cigarette. Hi, she said and half turned, playing mysterious but betraying herself with that smile, crude, sweet and perverse all at once. She was wearing an outfit of black leather, half trashy, half cowboy, decorated with tassels, also leather, which fluttered at her sides. She liked me looking at her that way, with a mixture of amazement and complicity, and she widened her smile to reveal all her teeth, releasing a mouthful of smoke.

'I've got the motorbike,' she said. 'Guido lent it to me for a few hours, until one.'

When I went back into the kitchen, Jaime was shaking up a fresh gourd of maté next to the kettle, which was engulfed in flames. Waiting for me to say something, playing dumb. I didn't say anything, I went into the bathroom and peed quickly, splashed my face with cold water to wake me up, avoiding the mirror, and took two small jumps into the bedroom to put on the first thing I could find, without switching on the light.

'You're off out, then,' Jaime confirmed, testing the maté with a few preliminary sucks at the straw.

'For a while,' I said, 'just for a ride.'

And I added:

'Her brother lent her the motorbike.'

Jaime overemphasised a sigh, his eyes loaded with irony, as if he were obliged to be happy about it too.

The motorbike's headlight suddenly hit me face on. I felt my way forward a few metres, dazzled by the ring of light that refused to be eclipsed by my body.

'Are you going like that?' Eloísa complained from the darkness.

'What do you mean, like that?'

'With that blouse.'

'What's wrong with it?'

'I don't know, it's a bit strange, a bit old.'

She was right, this fabric printed with red and yellow roses didn't go very well with her attire. I hadn't noticed, but now that I could see myself properly, it did look a bit strange, as if from another era, a bit American Midwest. Let's go, I said, it's night-time, who's going to notice?

Eloísa offered me the only helmet she had. I put it on without thinking. We drove through the village at full speed, without exchanging a single word. I let her take me, putting my arms around her waist, my head compressed, my feet almost constantly in the air, unable to stay put on the footrests for long.

We came out onto the main road. Eloísa livened up. She drove safely, a bit madly, but safely. Several times she over-took the cars in front, so that those coming in the opposite direction flashed their lights at us. Pure adrenaline.

In the middle of nowhere, who knows where, Eloísa stopped the motorbike on the verge.

'How's it going? All right back there?'

I nodded the helmet. Eloísa took out a pre-rolled joint from one of the pockets of her leather suit. She looked like a guy.

'Later I'm going to call Guido and tell him that we ran out of fuel and we've got no readies . . .' she said, drowning the last word in a first noisy drag. 'Then we can go home when we want.'

I laughed. I don't know why. She did too. We smoked the joint in less than three minutes, without speaking. We were in a hurry.

The rest of the journey was a wild race, a race with certain obstacles that Eloísa took great care to avoid, as if it were a matter of life and death. Cars, lorries, barriers, traffic lights and even the signals of a policeman at a road patrol: Eloísa kept going, braking only when she had to, it was all a matter of looking ahead.

We went through the centre of Pilar in search of a bar that Eloísa knew. She had been there once, but she couldn't remember exactly where it was.

'Of course, I was very drunk when I left,' she explained and let out a cackle as she turned to face forwards again.

Eventually we found it. The place was a long corridor: on the right, a string of tables seating two or three, on the left, a bar with a series of swivelling stools attached to the floor and, at the back, a circular dance floor. A blackboard announced happy hour until midnight. It wasn't even ten, we had more than enough time.

'Two fernet and cokes,' said Eloísa without asking me.

There was a basketball game being shown on the telly, which, as we discovered later, was the world final. For a good while, as the drinks flowed, we followed the ups and downs of the game quite attentively and it turned out to be much more entertaining than I would ever have thought.

We got drunk quickly. Meanwhile, the bar emptied and, in less than an hour, filled up again with new people. Couples, groups of three or four boys, groups of girls, more numerous, up to five or six, mostly teenagers. Eloísa was excited by what was going on around her and didn't ever call Guido to tell him about the bike. At some point, two lads of no more than eighteen approached us, without much conviction. Hi, said one. Can we sit down, asked the other. And Eloísa, who's an expert in these things, sent them packing with three words: We're fine, thanks, she said. The boys looked at each other, they laughed and left.

A few minutes before twelve, Eloísa drew a circle in the air around our drinks with her index finger, then pointed upwards. The barman understood immediately: another round of fernet, just in time to make the most of happy hour. The barman was almost completely bald, twice as old as the oldest person in the bar at that moment. Tanned skin, a ring through his left earlobe, bulging, green eyes, spanned by one single brow, and a faded denim shirt that he surely must have worn when he still had hair.

We spent a good while discussing whether Eloísa should stay in Open Door or move to the capital. Both options had their pros and cons. I was losing the thread of the conversation a bit. Every so often, the barman approached us, throwing some comment in the air for our entertainment. Initially Eloísa was aloof, but eventually, I don't know exactly when, she began to laugh at the guy's nonsense.

I went to the toilets to sober up a bit. I spent something like ten minutes sitting on a lavatory with the cubicle door locked shut. Three girls of fifteen or sixteen had installed themselves in front of the mirror to touch up their make-up, fix their hair and do some lines of coke. And they talked about it, about how they felt, about the drug, about what it did to you. One of them, the quietest, had never snorted cocaine. The other two convinced her with all kinds of arguments.

That nothing bad would happen, that it was like a buzz, that she would feel different, really alert. I didn't want to leave my cubicle. I didn't want to see their faces, or surprise them, so I decided to wait until they left.

In the bar, Eloísa and the barman were arm wrestling. For an instant, I didn't know whether to join them or keep going. I kept going. I sat on a chair near the entrance, next to a table filled with empty beer bottles. I needed some air. I closed my eyes for a while, without falling completely asleep. Until I fell completely asleep.

When I woke, the place was full. Around me, I saw only pieces of bodies, backs, arms, legs, all squashed up against each other, like on a Japanese metro.

I left the bar. It was gone four-thirty. The motorbike was still there, chained to a lamp post. I settled myself on the seat, resigned to giving her all the time in the world. But no: Eloísa appeared in a few minutes. She came from behind and covered my eyes with her hands.

Bet you can't guess where I've been, she said, but I was too tired and left her hanging.

Without a helmet and the wind full in my face, the return journey seemed much shorter than the way there. At the roadside, a dense layer of mist overshadowed the country-side: pure phantasmagoria.

Arriving in Open Door, as the combination of the joint, alcohol and exhaustion was conspiring in my head and my only concern was finding something to swallow to lessen my headache and getting to sleep as soon as possible, Eloísa accelerated and turned round to give me a kiss. We were at the level crossing. She kissed me, and we went flying.

I opened my eyes, scratching at the dirt in the deep ditch. I was shaking. The first thing I saw were the giant silos silhouetted in the night, too close. I wanted to take off the helmet but I wasn't wearing it. It was my head that weighed so heavily. I bit wet grass and filled my lungs with cold, corrosive air. I had the feeling that if I stretched out my arm I could grab the handlebars of the motorbike, fallen on the tarmac. The bike blocked my view of everything else. I pulled myself up slightly. What I hadn't been able to see was two bodies. Two inert bodies, one close by, the other further away. Two bodies instead of one. The body closest to me began to move, right in the middle of the road, encased in black leather. The other raised its head and part of its chest above the edge of the ditch, in a perfectly straight line in front of me. Eloísa finished raising herself and sat where she was, her gaze lost in the direction of the colony. I brought my legs together very slowly and drew them in towards me, tentatively, as if they were someone else's. My right knee was skinned to a fiery red. Now I understood the word burn.

We got up at the same time, lacking the courage to look at each other and, together, we approached the other, unexplained body. It was an older man, about Jaime's age, or more. The little hair he had was tousled, his arms hidden under his chest, his shoes submerged in a pool of mud and his mouth half open in a rigid, disgusted grimace. Eloísa hugged me, sobbing, reminding me that she was just a girl.

The man was breathing. In truth, he was blowing and each gasp shook the blades of grass that were moulded onto his face. Suddenly he let out a thin whine followed by a convulsion. He opened his eyes. Two deep wells, injected with all the blood in his head. He stared at us, embarrassed. He was short and solidly built. He was in a bad way, on his last legs. He couldn't have been drunker. When he tried to stand, he nearly lost his balance and fell. But he righted himself immediately, standing firm with his feet on the bed of the channel, and rummaged in his trouser pockets for a crushed packet of cigarettes, which he patiently moulded back into shape. He removed one, asked for a light with a clumsy gesture and took a couple of drags, looking around him aimlessly. Eloísa peeled herself off me, calm once more. The man was about to speak. Eloísa looked for her own packet of cigarettes, she asked me for a light as well and the two glowing embers gave us a little light.

TWENTY-SEVEN

Huret. Lunatics, work and play.

'As far as the lunatics' regime is concerned, it consists of mild and abundant food, agreeable work and recreation, walks, games in the open air, indoor games, theatre, dances, cinema, etc.

'All the lunatics work according to their capabilities and skills, provided they wish to do so. They are not forced to work. They may be encouraged, where possible, with the promise of a reward to their taste, for example tobacco. And indeed work is one of the principal elements of the cure. Some occupy themselves making brooms, others apply themselves to carpentry; bricklayers work at their trade. A French gardener, also a lunatic, creates flowerbeds in front of our eyes. Blacksmiths, locksmiths, carpenters, tailors and bakers work from morning to night, some single-mindedly, others dreaming, according to the temperament of each.'

It was my birthday yesterday and Jaime gave me a Walkman. I wasn't going to tell him, but later it occurred to me that perhaps it would improve the relationship and make him forget about the incident with Eloísa. And so it was. We need to celebrate, he said, with the widest smile I've ever seen on his face. He called the hospital and told them that he wouldn't be going in because his lawnmower was broken. We got into the truck, crossed the village and joined the main road.

'I want to apologise for the other day,' says Jaime, 'the thing with the girl, it was nonsense, you're right, she's just a kid, she can't be more than fifteen, right?'

He spoke without looking at me, his fingers interlaced at the top of the steering wheel, eyes glued to the tarmac. He took advantage of a short silence to overtake a tractor that was driving with two wheels on the verge and the other two on the road, and concluded:

'You get these silly things in your head and you can waste your whole life on this stuff.' Jaime drove on happily, proud of what he had just said.

We must have covered about 20 kilometres when, after passing a deserted level crossing, Jaime left the main road. He turned onto a gravel track that opened up without warning on the left and in less than a minute we were surrounded by countryside. Still silent, biting back an anxious smile, he accelerated as much as the engine would allow, using the rattling noises to keep the surprise he'd prepared for me under wraps. We paused for a few seconds at the foot of a slope the truck struggled to climb and when we arrived at the top, an immense lake appeared in front of us, filling the entire landscape. Jaime relaxed, and I thanked him for the present with a kiss on the cheek. We went on a few metres

and stopped next to a brick hut, as precarious as it was unlikely. I'll be right back, said Jaime and reappeared a few minutes later with a bottle in one hand, half a loaf of bread and
an extremely long salami in the other.

'Local wine, farmhouse bread and handmade salami,' he
said, holding up our lunch on the other side of the window.

We ate our picnic by the lake and I told myself again
that, despite everything, he was a good man and if I wanted
to I could still fall in love with him.

On the return trip, Jaime insisted on giving me a
present.

'I don't know, I can't think of anything,' I said honestly.

'There must be something, something you like or
need.'

I indulged him and said that I wanted a Walkman.

'To listen to music while I'm out walking,' I explained.

For an instant, Jaime fell silent, as if I'd said something
wrong, something offensive. But he quickly became himself
again.

'Let's go to the shopping centre,' he said, seriously, 'they
must have one there.'

After the shopping centre, we returned to the farm, made
love and slept a long siesta that lasted until quarter to seven.
I woke up suddenly, frightened. Jaime was sprawled across
the bed, one foot imprisoning my right leg. The bedside lamp
next to him was switched on. I extracted my leg carefully,
trying not to wake him, and left the room with my sandals
in my hand. On the kitchen table was a package that for a

moment I didn't recognise. It was the Walkman in its box, still wrapped and unused. It made me happy to think that it was still my birthday and that there was still time to visit Eloísa and tell her. She would surely suggest a toast, almost certainly with beer.

I'd had a nice day, better than I expected, especially since I hadn't expected anything at all. I thought about the lake, the wine and the salami, the return journey, the trip to the shopping centre in search of my present, that fantastic hour spent comparing Walkmans, the cake and coffee in the food court, the cloud of dust raised by the truck as we passed the door of the shop, the afternoon of calm sex, Jaime's expression, a smile on his face all day. I opened the box, discarding the instruction manual, and unrolled the headphone cables, connected it and switched it on. Nothing, not even a hum, utter silence. I pressed all the buttons without achieving anything. It took me a long minute to think of batteries. I checked in all the drawers. I found candles, rolls of tinfoil, red envelopes of rat poison, two identical lighters, a box with a few toothpicks, a load of corks, playing cards, bits of steel wool, screws, three loose cloves of garlic, a paintbrush, more poison and not a single battery. I was on the verge of giving up when I lifted my gaze and by chance saw a mini juicer, practically a toy, which Jaime had bought a few weeks ago for me to make orange juice. I dismantled it in seconds and took the batteries.

I turned the dial from one end to the other a couple of times until I found a station playing old favourites, themes from the sixties, seventies and eighties. *All-time classics,* the programme was called. I wrapped myself in the throw that covered the armchair and ventured out under the newly darkened skies. I had forgotten that sensation of cosmic plenitude that you get when you walk to your own music. I circled the house, stopped next to the mill and counted the first stars. It was one of those nights that you get only in the countryside. I felt peaceful.

I was suddenly distracted by something, a white, restless light, coming from the stable. The stable lights were yellow. And since the fire, Jaime hadn't even switched them on. I moved back a few metres. I looked away for a second and when I turned my head again, the light had disappeared. The same thing happened again twice, a strange light, meaningless, appearing and disappearing. I approached fearlessly. The stable door was ajar, the chain hanging from one of the handles. Too close now, the light surprised me again. A reflex made me hide behind one of the stalls. The ring of light was moving more and more frenetically. I climbed onto a bale of straw and leaned towards an opening halfway between the stall and the floor.

Boca was standing right in front of me, one hand holding a flashlight, which shook ceaselessly, the other clinging to a post. With her back to me, crouching down, Eloísa's head was jerking away at the level of the old man's prick. I couldn't tell who was abusing whom.

I masturbated furiously, along with the two of them. After they left, I waited a few minutes before climbing off the bale. Only now did I realise that the Walkman was still on and I'd been listening to music all this time. Unaware.

TWENTY-EIGHT

Aída's ghost appeared to me in the middle of the night, right underneath the crucifix, her back against the wall, inoffensive. I didn't attach any great importance to it, I put it down to tiredness, to the countryside and its inventions. She looked thin, not at her best, but underneath it all quite well.

It's an incredible, sun-filled morning and all the colours are alive and vivid, it feels as though spring has taken a step forward. I return to the library to thank Brenda for the translation. It's really just an excuse to see her again and try to unravel the intrigue that has begun to build around her. As soon as I open the door, I hear her voice. She's speaking loquaciously and animatedly in a room at the side. I lean in and see her surrounded by three boys in school overalls, aged between eleven and thirteen, who are listening reasonably attentively. I spy on them. She's talking to them about antiquity, about Athens, the Parthenon, the Roman

Empire and she hands them a heavy, brown volume of an encyclopaedia, which they receive somewhat fearfully, warily. I retrace my steps to the entrance, I don't want them to discover me. There are two books piled on Brenda's desk, one in English, the other in Spanish: *Billy Bathgate* by E. L. Doctorow and *Gods and Heroes* by Gustav Schwab. The former has all the appearance of a bestseller. When Brenda sees me, she greets me with a smile that erases whatever might have happened the last time. There are no traces of the wounds on her ears.

'I've got something for you,' she says and hands me a photocopy. 'I thought you might be interested.'

I read it out loud, for both of us:

'Today is a memorable day in the annals of public healthcare for the insane in our country, as we comply with the National Law of October 2nd, 1897, which orders the creation of an asylum for the mentally ill, according to the Scottish system known as open door, destined to fundamentally alter the care of these patients.

'We pray, then, Señor Presidente, ladies and gentlemen, that this establishment, the first and most advanced in South America, might open its doors as soon as possible for the scientific treatment of patients from the entire Republic who currently lack this care, achieving as such a progression worthy of the social culture of our nation.'

Words of the inaugural speech of the National Colony for the Insane, spoken by Dr Domingo Cabred on May 21st, 1899.

Some way from the house, on the other side of the fence, Eloísa and little Martín, Boca's nephew, pass by. They walk side-by-side; I can make them out clearly in spite of the distance. I wonder whether they'll see me. Now they disappear behind the pampas grass, heading towards the lake.

TWENTY-NINE

There are nights when I flop on my back in the grass and the sky leaves me speechless. It's a feeling that lasts for a few minutes and is then undone, either through distraction or sadness. In a second, I come and go from this state of almost pure amazement to a kind of complicated introspection. These things happen more in the country than in the city: this is what happens to town folk when they go into the countryside.

Jaime had gone to bed early, he wasn't feeling very well. I was in the middle of my star-gazing when Eloísa took me by surprise, scaring me a bit. She said that she'd come to get me to go for a wander. Of course, I didn't mention the episode in the stable, although I couldn't get it out of my head, try as I might.

In spite of the rain over the last few days, an unexpected heat had arrived, with mosquitoes and everything. We were on the veranda and Eloísa tried to convince me to borrow the pick-up for a couple of hours.

'He'll never find out, if nobody tells him, he's got no reason to find out,' she says.

'It's lunacy,' I reply, just to say something.

But she doesn't give in, she annoys me, she plays the capricious teenager. It's quarter to twelve and the air is still, stagnant, like a low storm cloud skimming the ground, crawling with fireflies and crickets, synchronised in a mathematical counterpoint, a precise second separating the sparks of some from the screeches of others. No, I tell her. No, and stop bugging me. I want to make her understand my reasons but it's impossible:

'He'll have a fit if he hears the engine,' I say.

'Come on,' she says. 'Let's go and have fun for a while, then we'll come back, there's nothing wrong with that.'

Eloísa stays quiet, watching me, like an obedient dog, and her last words ricochet gently through my mind. Come on: her eyes repeat. And that gaze hypnotises me, makes me feel like a nail caught in a magnetic field, with those furious eyes of a perverse child. That's it, an obedient dog with furious eyes. Everything changes in a fraction of a second with that short, simple sentence, 'let's go and have fun for a while,' it runs through my body like a potent drug, it becomes a perfect logic, a duty. That's the way it goes, it's stupid, things reveal their other side, their imminent side. Like that brat, who appeared at just the right time, that uncouth little brat, beautiful and elemental, who I can only think about touching, touching and touching, and yes, we need to have fun, let's go and have fun for a while and then we'll come back.

'Let's go,' I say and between us we come up with a brilliant idea to avoid waking Jaime. We need to push the truck as far as the gate and start the engine there.

Eloísa waits on the veranda rolling a joint while I enter the house on my tiptoes and slink with catlike movements towards the bedroom. I use two fingers to half open the door, keeping my breathing to a minimum, three short steps to the bedside table on Jaime's side, I skim my hand across the surface with the greatest of delicacy, identify the bunch of keys, pick it up in three silent beats, and retrace my steps. Jaime snores softly with his trousers on, unconscious. I get dressed in the dark, using the doorframe for balance, I put on jeans, a white t-shirt and grab the two pairs of rubber boots that are always in the corner of the wardrobe. Now that I'm outside, as I wipe the sweat from my forehead with the back of my hand, I peek through the keyhole: nothing, utter darkness, nothing to indicate that Jaime has found out. I feel like the perfect thief.

Outside, Eloísa has already smoked half the joint, but you can't tell, she's impervious to it, so she says. I put on Jaime's yellow boots, Eloísa wears mine. Both of us find them too big.

Eloísa grabs the keys of the truck from me. I take a few moments to draw in what's left of the joint and catch up with her. Eloísa releases the handbrake and moves the gear lever into neutral. She knows what she's doing. Without closing the door, she clings onto the window frame and signals for me to push.

Reaching the gate is an odyssey full of mud, slips, falls and laughter, stifled to avoid waking Jaime. It's madness, it's pointless, I repeat in my head, laughing to myself a bit. The joint is certainly having an effect on me.

We can't go on, we run out of strength a few metres from the gate. By mutual agreement we lie down in the back of the pick-up, facing the stars. The sky has cleared but the moon can't be seen. Eloísa takes out another joint. We smoke in silence, two drags each until it's finished. And now, I can't move. I close my eyes, whatever happens, happens.

Eloísa finds energy from somewhere; she always has something left. I can't see her, but I know that she gets up and starts jumping on the floor of the truck, making my head explode. Then she calms down, she moves about, she intrigues me.

A minute or an hour later, a cool breeze makes the hairs on my legs stand on end. I can't remember the last time I shaved them, not to mention further up. I'm not wearing my trousers any more, or my knickers. I'm about to open my eyes, but Eloísa gives me no time, with her tongue she wets those hollows that hide between my cunt and the top of my legs, the right and the left, first one, then the other. She moves away slightly, pauses, and blows, filling me with her fiery breath, she moves away again: she's becoming an expert. She has method. But then she loses herself and charges with everything she has, like an animal, licking me from my arsehole to the tip of my clitoris, hungry, disoriented, and she puts her fingers inside me, one, two, as many as she can fit. Another pause, and she asks me sarcastically: Do you want me to go on? And I turn into a single inarticulate plea, incapable of saying a word. We're in the middle of the countryside. Then she continues, more frenetically than before, and there was I thinking there couldn't be any more. She swallows me, eats me, tears me to pieces. I open my eyes and finish off howling like a madwoman.

At dawn, the rain returned and erased the tracks that the tyres had left between the house and the gate. Jaime tried to find a way to explain the truck's mysterious journey.

'Perhaps I've caught something with all those loonies around me, but I could have sworn that I left it right here,' he said and we both laughed.

When I wake up, Boca is already doing the barbecue. He's with a girl of around Eloísa's age. But later, throughout the day, during the meal and as we chat afterwards, he treats her as if she were his wife. Where on earth does Boca find his teenage girlfriends?

THIRTY

I woke up vomiting. Jaime, being used to Boca who, when he overdoes the wine and meat, goes off somewhere into open country, puts two fingers down his throat and returns it all to the earth, didn't make a big deal of it. Boca returns and explains, even though he doesn't need to: I let it all out. And sometimes he adds: I'm good as new, or Nothing to see here. Jaime contains his laughter, pressing his lips together like a teenager. He's his accomplice. Once they hit fifty, men are either too solitary or together too much, like adolescents. Sometimes self-absorbed and ill-tempered, sometimes extroverted and bloody annoying.

Every other Saturday, Jaime and Boca go hunting in the woods. At around two in the morning, after a long barbecue and lots of preparation, they load their rifles and ammunition into the back of the pick-up and disappear into the night. They hardly ever bring anything back. Sometimes they return straight away, other times dawn breaks and they still haven't appeared. What do they do? Shoot? Get drunk? Have sex? Without witnesses, anything is possible.

Eloísa appears with Loti, leading him by the hand. She whistles from the gate, she doesn't want to come in. I don't feel like going but curiosity, jealousy and boredom impel me. With the gate between us, Eloísa makes the introductions. She says our names and smiles, her lips sparkling. Loti is tall, very slim, with delicate yet virile features. His eyes are such a deep blue that they almost seem fake, and his teeth are small, brown and small. But what makes Loti an unquestionable gypsy are his hands. They need no further description, they're gypsy hands. Eloísa doesn't know what to say. She came to show me her Romanian, as hunters show off their catch, proudly. He's her new toy. Loti watches her, besotted, rather lost, either because he likes her a lot or because he doesn't understand a word she says.

Aída, or her ghost, appears to me more and more often, at any time of day, under any pretext, usually in the kitchen. She even goes so far as to sit at the table, between Jaime and me, but I stay quiet, I act as if nothing's happening, so as not to disturb Jaime. I get used to it.

THIRTY-ONE

'Would you believe me if I said that there are no more than fifty people in Buenos Aires who know of Open Door?' Domingo Cabred to Jules Huret.

Guido's birthday party took place in the grocery storeroom, surrounded by bags of flour, packets of espadrilles, tools, bags of coal, bundles of wood, giant aluminium pans, all sorts of tins, toys, piles of gardening gloves and a multitude of dust-coated bottles of *aguardiente*. The same stuff I'd seen displayed on the shelves of the shop, but in bulk and with that nightmarish quality that things have when they are too many to count.

Eloísa came to get me at ten. I'm going, I said. At the same time, or a couple of seconds later, Jaime opened the tap and put a pan containing the remains of dinner underneath the jet of water just to make noise and not have to hear me. Eloísa had gone into the bedroom without asking permission, as if it belonged to her. I persisted. Jaime, I'm going. He answered with more noise, banging the plates and cutlery he had to hand, playing deaf like an offended child. I felt sorry for him.

Eloísa appeared on tiptoes in one of my dresses. What do you think? she said, extending her arms above her head, full of life. Jaime turned off the tap, looked round and raised his shoulders, nose and eyebrows, biting his tongue to hide his surprise. It was a skin-coloured dress, made of a very fine fabric, semi-transparent, and it definitely looked better on her than it did on me. Jaime opened the tap again and spoke with his back to us.

'I'm going out too, take your keys,' he said.

It's a perfect night, said Eloísa and took out a fat joint that she'd already rolled, which we finished quickly, before we even passed the gate. The rest of the way, neither of us opened our mouths. We were in a hurry, anxious. She wasn't the same Eloísa as in the early days. More grown up, or sadder, she kept things to herself.

The door of the storeroom was decorated with a garland and a string of flashing Christmas-tree lights that intertwined to form an arch. When we arrived, Guido was busy placing bottles of beer in some buckets of ice. It was early. People will start coming around twelve, he said.

The first to arrive was Armando, a pleasant, funny boy, with more pimples than face. Then the rest started piling in. The party started properly when a group of six girls arrived, among whom was Dani, a little blonde girl with short hair who Eloísa pointed out as Guido's sort-of-girlfriend. The last to arrive was Moncho, who made us all go outside to admire the motocross bike he'd just been given. It's the business, said Guido.

At about half one, some people started dancing to keep warm. Guido, Moncho, Eloísa and two other partygoers were having a 'down in one' contest, emptying their glasses with that unique speed possessed only by teenagers. Eloísa kept winning, it was obvious that they were letting her. She knew it and she liked it. I felt a bit left out, from another generation. Moncho took me up to dance, and I let myself be taken.

Later, the party extended into the shop itself, using the old wooden counter as a bar. The boys danced in a circle, and every so often one or other of them would step into the middle to play the fool. Eloísa started dancing alone, like a madwoman, attempting a sensual choreography, which to me, looking in from the outside, the effects of the marijuana having worn off, seemed pathetic. Disappointed, or frightened, the other girls, including the little blonde who had barely exchanged a word with Guido, were gradually starting to leave. I went outside as well, for some air. The night, moonless, was a dark cell.

When I returned to the shop, Eloísa was dancing in the middle of a circle of five or six boys, including Guido. When she saw me, she broke the ring, pulling me towards her into the centre of the circle. I resisted slightly and she didn't insist. Eloísa returned to the bullring. An anonymous push planted Guido face-to-face with his sister, who at the least touch broke into a frenetic dance. Guido decided to pretend he was groping her, without actually touching her, like an aspiring mime artist. Eloísa raised her bum and stuck out her small tits to meet her brother's indecisive hands. Guido was doing it for his friends, Eloísa for me, like two kids playing for their parents' approval. Guido's friends were cheering like degenerates, some giving high-pitched howls, like wolf cubs. One of them suggested: They should kiss. And immediately, the crowd roared its approval. That said it all. I joined the circle and the chorus: Kiss, kiss, kiss, kiss. Since Guido was laughing without doing anything, the group resigned itself to something lesser and the chorus requested a peck instead. Eloísa took the initiative: she shook her brother by the shoulders – by this stage he looked like a scarecrow dazed by the fluttering of a flock of birds – and planted a wet kiss on his incredulous mouth. An animalistic, endless kiss. Guido went white, his friends stopped applauding, their eyes popping out of their heads.

Moncho was the first to react, he stepped forward a few paces, and started dancing behind Eloísa, grabbing her round the waist, and the others, still stupefied, began clapping again.

Between Guido and Moncho, with a movement that would be impossible to reconstruct, so agile, so dreamlike, Eloísa bent down with all the voracity she could muster. Moncho thought he knew what was coming and despite his doubts, he unzipped his trousers. But Eloísa managed the situation perfectly, she knew what she wanted and in another of those magical movements that left everyone feeling rather foolish and open-mouthed, she undressed her brother from the waist down and began caressing him with both hands. Guido squeezed his eyelids shut so as not to see, Moncho groped Eloísa's tits thinking that he would be next. But no, he would be left hanging, the same as Guido who was so nervous that he couldn't relax at all. Eloísa looked up at her brother from below, stroking his flaccid cock, and forgave him with a smile full of kindness. She broke the circle, grabbed me by the hand and pulled me into the storeroom to unburden herself.

'It's just a joke,' she said in my ear, 'don't get annoyed.'

THIRTY-TWO

Now the ghost speaks, she says things, incongruous things, sometimes she complains, other times she laughs, it's a forced laugh, wasted on alcohol. There's something different in the timbre of the voice, but it's her, as if in flesh and blood. I try to ignore her, to convince myself that it's just my imagination, a demented, perverse game, that my subconscious is subjecting me to tests to keep me on my toes, and yet it's so convincing, so real, that I don't want to even think about stretching out my arm: what if I touch her?

I wonder whether it wouldn't be a good idea to talk to someone about it, but with whom, it's madness, just think of Jaime's expression if I told him.

On Saturday morning, Jaime goes to Luján to buy a new scythe. The other one is no good anymore, he says, I can't even sharpen it. I go with him. He parks the truck in the centre of town, in front of the basilica. We agree to meet back here in an hour, at half twelve. If you want, we can grab something to eat afterwards. In the doorway of the church, there are two or three stalls brimming with effigies of the Virgin Mary. There are wooden virgins half a metre tall, hard plastic ones, wax versions with a wick at the top, plug-in virgins with long cables and bulbs inside, paper virgins, and lots of predictive virgins, like toy barometers, that change colour depending on the weather. Blue: good. Violet: changeable. Pink: rainy. Most of the virgins, except for one or two that must be broken, are violet and yet the sky is overcast with clouds that are closer to black than grey and look ready to burst at any moment. Without my asking, as I study one of the statuettes to try to discover its secret and its fault, the stallholder explains that the little virgins, as she calls them, also work inside. Great.

It's almost twelve, I head towards the truck. First, I drop into a vet's surgery and ask for a bottle of ketamine. They look at me strangely and ask for a prescription. I show a credential, which I have with me by chance.

Later, Eloísa confesses what I already knew. She tells me that she slept with little Martín, that she did it because she felt sorry for him. She wants to know if I'm annoyed.

THIRTY-THREE

'It's very strange, I know that it makes no sense, but it's starting to worry me more than it should, and I need to tell someone about it . . .' I say to Yasky as we walk around the polo field; I choose my words carefully so that he doesn't think I'm crazy. I break off, I pause, I'm not entirely sure about telling him, there's still time to backtrack and invent something else. But no, I tell him all at once, to take the weight off my shoulders and exorcise the ghost.

'For a while now I've been having a kind of vision, very tangible and real . . . Aída, my friend, the girl from the bridge, appears to me every now and then, anywhere, and she speaks, she talks to me . . .' I finish speaking and cover my mouth to stop myself laughing.

Yasky leaves without saying anything to placate me. I feel lost.

The Romanians' ranch was burnt down. I find out from Boca.

The police scour the surrounding area but there's no one left. They're used to fleeing, they're gypsies in spirit. I wonder what will become of Loti, whether we'll see him again. I hope not.

We spend the whole night taking ket, like two madwomen. Talking ceaselessly, without listening to each other, coming and going to the bathroom. Hard like two hard mares. We drink half a demijohn of wine. Without touching each other, or kissing; in another world.

When we began to run out of air, Eloísa opened the door of the storeroom slightly and the morning hit us in the face, just the same as every other morning, except that, for the first time, it was spinning like a giant, straying top. We went outside for a walk. We crossed the sleeping village, as far as the train tracks. Elo said that she didn't feel well. My heart's beating too fast, she said. Her breathing was agitated. Her forehead was covered in droplets of sweat. I touched her back. You're soaking wet. What are we going to do? It's, like, nine and I've got to call home, I say. And her: Stop fucking about. You're going mad, that house is murder. Eloísa started walking in no particular direction with her heart leaping out of her body. I stayed where I was, weak and sleepless. I remained like that for some time, my mind blank, until the truck appeared and filled my eyes with dust. The door opened and Jaime waited patiently until I decided to climb in. The entire way home without talking or looking at each other, the radio on. I shut myself in the bedroom and slept until ten at night.

•

Now we're in the kitchen and the situation is confused, the furniture has changed places. Yasky speaks, explaining the facts. I settle down behind him, in the rearguard, I don't want to take charge. Jaime listens seriously, his fingers intertwined, pressing his thumbs together. One of his cigarettes hangs from his mouth, he expels smoke through his nose, with a defeated look on his face. He's not surprised by what he hears, he's annoyed. In spite of him, the talk is of ghosts and supernatural matters. Yasky says he has the solution, he proposes a session.

'There are methods,' says Yasky. 'Fairly effective methods, if you both agree, I can raise a request and ask for authorisation, or perhaps we don't need to, we could always organise a session between us, a conclave, in secret, right now.'

In addition to Yasky, there are two other men, one blond with earphones, the operator, and a tall, skinny guy, the witness, who will remain standing and silent throughout the session, lighting a fresh cigarette with the butt of the previous one.

We congregate around a strange device, like a portable mixing desk. Jaime, Yasky, Eloísa, the operator, the witness and me, in that order, in a clockwise direction. When did Eloísa appear? And what is she doing sitting on my knee? I have no answer to that. She seems happy, eager to find out what might happen. The operator presses a button, turns some knobs, the machine starts up. I'm well aware that we are in the presence of a ghost-catcher, the kind you used to get in the old days. Now, except for the witness, we're all wearing earphones like the operator's, although not quite so sophisticated. Jaime becomes tangled in the cables, he struggles to manoeuvre the equipment and Eloísa laughs in his face. She's stoned, it shows in her eyes, she must have smoked a joint on the way over. Now that I look closely, her blouse is undone, her tits on show, but nobody notices, it doesn't attract anyone's attention. The girl has no limits. The operator puts on some thin gloves, very fine and surgical-looking. Eloísa wants to touch all the buttons, I have to hold down her hands, she behaves just like a child, the operator looks at us furiously. But deep down he likes her, he's charmed by her.

We spend the whole night waiting for some kind of sign, a gesture, but since nothing happens, or else the machine isn't working, Boca, who all this time has been guarding the kitchen door with his gun in his hands, 'shooting ducks', as I thought I heard him say at one point, gets impatient and joins the witness who is setting out glasses to begin an old-style séance. Eloísa has fallen asleep under the table, curled up at my feet. Yasky tries to encourage us, Jaime has lost patience and every so often bangs the useless machine gently but nervously. The operator is confused, he feels small, he recognises his failure.

But the wait is justified. When we had already abandoned hope and were playing at making the glasses move around the tabletop, a sudden, painful, ultrasonic hum revives everyone's enthusiasm.

The spectre would manifest itself. The time had come. But something new happened, something unsatisfactory that put an end to everything. The device gave off some sparks, exploded and then plunged us into darkness.

THIRTY-FOUR

I spend my nights awake, reconstructing, with a bit of book-work and a lot of guesswork, the history of Open Door. I prefer to sleep during the day. In the daytime I don't dream. At night I do and the dreams, my recent dreams anyway, are too disturbing. I bought myself a cheap whisky that keeps me awake. Sometimes I wonder why I'm so interested in this particular story, when there are so many others; because it's close, because it's unlikely, because it's beginning to belong to me, because I have time on my hands, could it be because of Jaime, who I want to see less and less, or Eloísa, who I want to see more and more and who is driving me to distraction.

Very early, in secret, I submerge the tip in the piss-filled plastic container and leave it twice as long as the instructions suggest, to avoid any mistakes. It's the first pregnancy test I've done in my life. I never thought I'd actually be able to do it. They say that there are many reasons for periods being late: hormonal changes, mood swings, stress, traumatic situations, false pregnancies. There are women who go up to six months without menstruating for no obvious reason, on nature's whim, just because. Then out of the blue, it returns and they have normal periods again.

Late, but just how late? I'd lost track, but it was etched on my mind that the last one had arrived the day after that first night with Eloísa. I remembered it well because when I woke up that midday with Jaime's axe cracking a few metres from the window, I went to the bathroom to pee and the blood stains in my knickers filled me with sadness. Right then, it made no sense. My legs were still trembling, my head was still swimming from too many joints and so much crazy sex, deep sounds echoed in my ears and an exquisite tingling picked at the inside of my body. I could only think about when we would see each other again, that same night if possible. And in that instant, like a child betrayed by her own body, I thought that the blood had ruined everything.

That must have been the start of April, the first weekend of the month, the fourth or fifth, a few days after I started taking my unsuccessful trips to the morgue. And if a few weeks ago, when the idea began to spin round my head, it had seemed absurd, impossible, utter madness, later I convinced myself that yes, it was possible, I wasn't careful and although Jaime took precautions, they're never enough. The possibility tortured me: it struck me dumb for a couple of days. It even stopped me wanting to see Eloísa, as if I'd deceived her. But no, it made no sense. How many times had

I fucked without taking care and nothing had happened? It was all in my mind, and if my period hadn't arrived it was because I was changing, my body was speaking for me, I wasn't made to have children. And to stop me worrying over all these stupid speculations, the best idea was to confirm that it wasn't true. I'm not pregnant and that's the end of it.

Ready. I leave it a few seconds longer, my eyes following Jaime's presence as he gets lost on the way to the stable. It would be good for him to have another horse, not that he could replace the other Jaime, but at least what remains of the stable would stop being uninhabited and the heavy air that's starting to fill it with demons would be dispelled. Here I go: I take courage and pull the stick out of the container, which spills slightly over the toilet lid because my steady hand betrays me.

I make a note: *When Open Door was established in 1898, the lunatic population numbered 25; in 1912 it was 154; by 1925 it had reached 234 and they were no longer lunatics, they were internees, the mentally ill. In 2000 there are 1,964. An average of 65 new internees enter the institution every year.*

THIRTY-FIVE

This can't be right, I must be hallucinating. But no. I wake in the middle of the night between two deeply sleeping bodies, one face up, the other face down, Jaime on the right, Eloísa on the left. All three in the same bed. All three naked. The half-light makes me doubtful, but touch confirms what sight refuses to believe. My eyes cloud over: I don't know how we came to this.

Jaime had come home drunk, drunker than anyone I've ever seen, his mouth hanging open, fillings on show, upper teeth clashing against the lower. Dribbling all over himself. I remember that part perfectly.

He came in acting the way horses do when a lorry passes them on the road: randy. I'm hungry, he struggled to say as he kicked in the air to shake off his boots. I want to eat. I heated up some chicken soup left over from the night before. Jaime appeared from the bedroom, stooped and puffing, with an unfamiliar erection. And what happened next was so typical and so absurd that it didn't even hurt me. Jaime spat out the soup and right there, on the cold marble worktop, he mounted me, as a stallion would mount a mare, from behind, until he couldn't go on.

Then he left, he disappeared, and in a while Eloísa arrived, also pretty out of it. I told her that I didn't feel well and she massaged me and I her, and we must have fallen asleep without realising it.

I have no idea exactly when Jaime came in or how he managed to lie down without realising that Eloísa was in the bed. Or else he saw her and was still so drunk he didn't care.

I have to do something quickly, right now, but I only come up with bad ideas. What if I try to sleep again and let whatever happens happen. I glance to either side and I still can't understand it. Jaime snorts loudly, sprawled across the bed, disrobed and disorderly. Who will wake next, it could be Eloísa and she'll go without anyone noticing. But if Jaime opens his eyes first there's no going back, it will be irreversible.

The first thing I do is to pinch Eloísa hesitantly on one arm, very gently. I persist, a bit harder, but she doesn't react. When I finally manage to wake her, I quickly cover her mouth with my hand and explain the situation with gestures. Disconcerted and desperate to burst out laughing, Eloísa puffs her cheeks out, the colour rises to her face, and she does her best to contain her cackles until she can't help but release a little gasp, which she thankfully manages to stifle before it reaches Jaime's ears. She doesn't look good, she's pale, drugged. What I must look like, I don't want to know. Very slowly, measuring each movement by the millimetre, we raise ourselves until we manage to get out of bed. Eloísa goes first, on tiptoe, and I follow, resting one finger on her back to guide myself in the darkness. We reach the door, Eloísa opens it slightly, only as much as she needs to and slinks out like a cat.

Before leaving the room, I look round to set my mind at rest and confirm that the nightmare is over, but Jaime's eyes, wide open, make me wobble and I lose balance. I hang onto the doorframe and expect the worst. It takes Jaime a moment to speak.

'Are you all right?' he asks and I don't know whether he's making fun of me, testing me or whether he genuinely didn't notice anything. Words fail me.

'Are you all right?' Jaime repeats and I laugh nervously, almost giving the game away.

'I'm thirsty,' I do my best to say and he turns over to continue sleeping, face down now.

It's true, I'm dying of thirst, I feel like someone has slit my throat.

Later that same day, Eloísa looks at me with different eyes, she suspects, or she knows. We sit next to the bare fig tree and smoke a small joint in silence. She seems serious, grown up, with dark circles under her eyes, very different. It's not the same Eloísa from a few months ago, not a shred of innocence is left in her face, and yet I want her so much. I can only think about kissing her, about her going down on me as soon as possible.

'I think I'm pregnant,' I say quickly, to relieve myself of the burden.

THIRTY-SIX

I did another two tests, different brands this time, always following the instructions to the letter, always with the first pee of the morning, and the stick always comes out the same: two pale pink stripes, nice and clear, one on top of the other. Sometimes the upper stripe isn't quite as intense as the lower, but there's no getting away from it, the leaflet promises that two lines are an unmistakable sign: 99.9% reliable. But it can't be true, there must be some mistake. It must be a dream, bad but fleeting.

Yasky sent a telegram: *NO NEWS ON THE CASE.* It's the only thing he puts. He doesn't mention ghosts. He's stopped phoning me, he must be embarrassed, after everything. Aída hasn't appeared again either, she obviously felt intimidated. Or it could be that I'm not calling to her anymore.

Three days with no sign of Eloísa. Guido says he thinks she

went to visit a cousin who lives on the coast, but he's not sure. She went just like that, without letting me know. I'm dying to know where she is, who she's with, if she's laughing, if she's thinking of me, if she's horny, if she's fucking, if she's like that with everyone. I can't take it. Just five minutes of relief and then long, endless, delicious hours, filling my mind with Eloísa.

Jaime doesn't show up either. He left suddenly, with no explanation. One afternoon as he returned from the hospital, he parked the truck outside the front door, came in without even registering me, and locked himself in the bathroom until the following morning. Four days passed like that, just like the first. He would arrive, lock himself in the bathroom until the next day and leave at dawn. On the fifth day, a Friday, at about six, the telephone rang. It was Boca. He said that Jaime was going to be late because a job had come up on a ranch near Luján. A small job that would take them a few hours, so he told me. A week has already gone by, with no word from Jaime. He's a big boy. I don't need to worry about him.

The food runs out, only half a bag of self-raising flour left in the cupboard. I have neither the cash nor the will to go out and buy anything. Without really thinking about it, I begin scraping the wall behind the headboard with my nails and bringing to my mouth pieces of plaster, which peel off without too much difficulty. It's pure inertia. I suck them unenthusiastically, the edges scratch the roof of my mouth. Now I feel able to do a bit more, and I start chewing them. Inside my mouth, the slivers of plaster break into smaller and smaller pieces, and eventually dissolve in contact with the hot saliva. The sensation is strange but pleasant. A bit like eating consecrated wafers, I don't know, I've never tried them, it just occurred to me.

Without Jaime and without Eloísa, the days become long and nights empty. I feel useless, with no desire to do anything. As if the only truth were this country house that destiny made mine, these old sticks of furniture, the loonies prowling too close by, the village turning its back on me in its eternal siesta, and this solitude. Like a bad dream that I've always been here, waiting.

In the meantime, I smoke all the remaining cannabis with unfamiliar voraciousness. Tired, horny, moving from the bed to the kitchen, bouncing, leaning on the walls or crawling. Suddenly, without warning, a stabbing pain in my stomach makes me double up. I don't make it to the bathroom and halfway there, spattering the bedroom wall, I bring up all the plaster. I find it so disgusting that I have to spend a long time spitting up a kind of transparent cream, and it leaves me limp.

I spend the whole day dozing in bed, in the dark. Outside it must be raining, or cold: it's always inhospitable outside. I'm starting to like all of this less and less. I spend the day alone. I don't move and at times, because I've smoked so much weed, as they call it in the country, my head just goes, I lose all sense, I'm spaced. Everything becomes dark, dense, gelatinous, it all goes through my fingers, which scratch at my skin, hard, they seem to pass through my flesh and, right there, I stop being, I stop acting, I let myself be taken, lying down, standing up, my stomach pressed against the basin of thick, cold, Pampas-style porcelain, and I don't stop, I laugh alone, I dance about, I shiver slightly, and my fingers don't stop, as if they weren't mine, rubbing my clitoris, my button, twisting the hairs that cover my cunt, rubbing and putting themselves inside me, one, two, three, as many as can fit, I'm sweating like mad, and the other fingers go into other parts, massaging my arse, moistening my anus with the juice that slides down the crease, and a little ochre pool, pretty and transparent, spreads over Jaime's sheets, which swallow what he won't, what disgusts him, and the smell of the country, of wet grass, of fireflies, of dry vines, the newly cut privets, and the fruit trees, the medlars, kumquats, figs, the smell of wet mud, the smell of pollen, all those smells, native smells, mixing with mine, boiling, like those of a cat on heat, a mad cat, unhinged, a cat who can't take any more, who crawls, who comes for the umpteenth time, wildly, with misty eyes, undone by myself.

At some point the phone rings. I don't have the strength to answer. I pull myself upright as best I can and pick up the receiver. It's Yasky, he says that he has to see me. I don't let him finish, I hang up. In a minute the phone rings again, I assume it's still Yasky, offended, but I hear a silence filled with street noise and then Jaime's choked voice, coughing before speaking. I'm in the capital, I'm with Boca, he says. And I tell him the truth: I don't feel too good, I woke up with

an upset stomach. I hear the sound of the city again, compet-
ing with Jaime's breathing, which sounds like the puffing of
a thoughtful animal. He's about to say something but hangs
up instead. He doesn't call again.

I dream of toads, skirts, orgies and horses.

THIRTY-SEVEN

Eloísa reappeared after two weeks, as if nothing had happened. She'd been in Buenos Aires, staying with a guy she had met in the bar in Pilar, the same place she took me that time. A respectable boy, well-off, who lives with his parents in one of the gated communities, but who acts the hard-man, the druggy, and plays bass in a rock group with four guys just like him, a bit full of themselves, but pretty cool. That's how Eloísa describes him. This boy took her to a squat, or what she thought was a squat in Calle Estados Unidos, where some six or seven girls and boys lived. According to Eloísa there were a lot of drugs going about and she's not sure, but she thinks they were cutting cocaine in a room at the back by the utility room. She didn't go in.

'There were two older girls, your age, who wandered round topless all day. They made me think about us, I was dying to be close to you, to touch you,' says Eloísa.

We spend all afternoon smoking in the store shed

behind the shop. Between joints, we have sex: wild, violent, without pleasure.

Eloísa asks me whether now that I'm pregnant we're going to stop seeing each other. She looks at my flat stomach. She strokes it. I think it's great, she says, although I'm quite shocked. Do you think it's all right, what we're doing? It's the first time that Eloísa has asked whether something is right or wrong, I thought it was only me who wondered about that kind of thing. But she immediately laughs and pinches my bum. It's a joke, she says. She does what she likes with me, she plays with my body and my thoughts. She's a little bitch.

'I don't understand what you're doing with that old man. It doesn't make sense,' she says, soaked with sweat, her mouth still tasting of sex. 'It's madness. If I didn't know you better I'd say you were wrong in the head.'

Dawn breaks. I start to get cold, a light but continuous shiver passes through my body. Pieces of burnt sky covered by a single, red, uniform cloud reach me through the rafters.

'Aren't you saying anything?'

Eloísa speaks very close to my face, far more seriously than usual, challenging me.

'This place is hell, why don't you have an abortion and stop kidding yourself you've still got time to think about it?'

I look her in the eye, I stroke her hair, she curls up in my arms, she apologises.

'I'm sorry,' she says, 'I'll say anything.'

All day alone in the house, devouring pieces of plaster, loose rendering from the wall behind the wardrobe. I resist as long as I can, but the impulse is stronger than me, unstoppable. It leaves me with a harsh, piquant taste in my mouth, inflaming my throat. How long can this go on?

THIRTY-EIGHT

Jaime is moving his mouth, as if speaking, but I can't hear a single word. I've just opened my eyes and the first thing I see is a mountain landscape with very tall pines that cover nearly the whole sky. It's hanging in the middle of a wall papered with flowers so small they make me dizzy and force me to shut my eyes again. I'm exhausted. I breathe deeply, dispel all the air through my nose and look again. I can't control my eyes, they open and shut in spite of me. Behind Jaime there's a window covered with white curtains and a bit further over, in a corner, a kind of metal clothes rack. Above my head there are two neon tubes stuck to the ceiling, one switched on, the other off. My feet itch, I would love to be able to scratch them. To my right, a fat lady in a pale blue apron is also moving her lips, she's standing up, and bit by bit, I begin to make out scraps of words.

Things suddenly become clear. I'm lying in a hospital bed, Jaime is talking to a nurse and immediately that other hospital I woke up in some months ago comes into my mind. This feels more or less the same.

I want to raise a hand to say here I am. My arm doesn't respond straight away and only when I manage to shake it with the minimum of energy do Jaime and the nurse stop talking and turn their full attention to me. They observe me silently for a few seconds, waiting for me to do something else, I don't know what.

Now Jaime moves closer and strokes my hand, still in the air, and places it back beside the other. I try to speak, to ask the first questions, but Jaime silences me by raising his index finger to his lips as nurses in posters do.

'Rest,' he says twice, 'stay calm.'

I spend what is left of the day lying in bed, Jaime entering and leaving the room without saying much. At one point, without wanting to, I find myself with a mirror. I've never seen myself looking so horrible. Night falls and I'm fully awake at last. A different nurse brings me a tray with a piece of skinless chicken on a cushion of runny mash and a jelly the colour of piss.

'Eat,' says Jaime, 'it'll do you good.'

The nurse presses a button and the headboard rises until I'm almost sitting up. The chicken, the mash and the jelly all have the same taste of nothing. I quickly swallow all I can, Jaime eats the rest.

'You fainted,' he begins to tell me, 'I found you in the kitchen. They're going to do some tests. They say that if everything's OK, you can leave tomorrow.'

The night seems eternal, it feels like morning will never come. My head is full of gaps. Every time Eloísa enters my mind, I think about something else to get rid of her quickly.

Jaime can't sleep either. He's sitting on an armchair by the side of the bed. Our eyes meet two or three times and we become rather idiotic, each of us with a load of questions that the other won't answer because we never do. At one point I'm on the verge of confessing what he's going to find out sooner or later, but I don't know how.

The next day, with the tests that say I'm pregnant stuffed safely in my trouser pocket, Jaime helps me to dress and pays the hospital bill.

On the way home, just after the level crossing, at almost the exact place we first met, Jaime says that I should have told him sooner. He says it in a whisper, embarrassed, and I don't know how to respond.

I don't want to even think about how things are going to be from now on.

THIRTY-NINE

Outside it's thundering, without raining. The thunderclaps are long. They grow, they draw out, they growl, they burst and they extinguish. Jaime managed to get me a computer a few days ago, an old model, but it works. The mouse only moves from side to side, so I need to touch the little ball every now and again to get it in the right place. The monitor is one of those you used to get, fourteen inches and convex. The image flickers and every so often the colours disappear, then suddenly return. The keyboard makes a lot of noise, but evenly. All the letters sound the same, the *a* is the same as the *l*, the *j* as the *s*, the same as the space bar, the comma, the full stop, the underscore, the brackets, all the same. It's a cacophonous language. Only the intensity and the rhythm change. I wonder whether Jaime can sleep with all this hammering. It would seem so. He's on his back with his hands crossed on his chest, serene. This paternity business has returned him to his old self, docile and melancholic, like the other Jaime.

Now it shows, my stomach is just beginning to separate me from the edge of the table. Only a few centimetres, it's almost imperceptible, but it shows. At least I notice it, and that short distance fills me with questions, it distracts me. If it's a boy, will Jaime want to call him Jaime, like him and the other Jaime? When should it start kicking? When will the cravings come? How late on can I abort? I don't know, I just wonder.

Yesterday I went to bed early, at around eleven; Jaime stayed in the kitchen smoking with the radio on. The dream came immediately, very clear, and either I was to blame for interrupting it, or it was the thirst that was scratching at my throat and drying the roof of my mouth until I could bear it no longer and woke up. If I'd had a pitcher of water to hand, who knows, perhaps the dream would have gone on.

It was a vast room, five metres by eight, a magnificent and luminous place. The flat is on a coastal avenue by the beach, second or third floor. The city is Rio de Janeiro. There's a white leather couch, extremely large, for four or five people, between two clear columns, which are actually fish-tanks full of bubbling water, with oxygen pumps but no fish. There's another armchair, with an anatomically shaped back and a footrest. And another, upholstered in cowhide, the fibres bristled with static, with a movable base so that it can rock. All the chairs are occupied by suntanned people, mainly twenty-something men, in light and frivolous clothing, their feet mostly bare and playful. They murmur but don't speak. They propose toasts and laugh. They seem happy. There are two or three, a woman, a man with very little hair, smooth-skinned and chubby-cheeked, and some-one else I can't see, who zigzag gently between the seats, and disappear down a long corridor full of pictures or pho-tographs of clouds, and I follow them until the point where they leave me. I stop outside a bathroom with no door, and a woman sitting on the toilet, wearing thick-framed, feline glasses, her trousers round her ankles, smiles at me, draws her knees together and leans forward: she's small. I haven't seen her before. I stay there for a few seconds, or longer, with-out annoying her, until she starts to pee. Then I get a bit lost, in the kitchen, in the bedrooms, too alone, until I'm back at the party.

Now the woman with glasses is leaning against one of the columns, rocking a baby in a nappy. The others are still there, sprawled on the chairs, drinks in hand, touching one another's feet. Erotic games. And, not really knowing how long I've been holding this rifle with a silencer and laser sight, I point it at the baby, resting the flickering, red circle on its forehead. No one protests, it's all normal. I change tar-get, from the baby to the man with hardly any hair, and I start swivelling round, marking all of them with the glowing ring, one by one: heads, legs, shoulders, pelvises, at random. It's insane, but it seems as though I'm going to kill them all.

Boca and Jaime are always playing *truco*, they never tire of it. Nor does it incite any great passion, they just play. They shuffle, deal, and speak only when necessary for the game to continue. And they keep a tally, point by point, dash by dash. There are no breaks, no half-time, it's a continual performance, no winner, no loser, a cyclical journey that leads nowhere. Nobody decides when it ends, it's an organic gesture: to play or not to play. I close in, I spy on them, I make faces at them, but they don't notice, I don't bother them. They raise the stakes, without risk or hesitation. Bean by bean. And me too, on the outside, although I'm not taking part in the game, I'm there, with them, half horny, half lonely, circling around them, and I'm part of it, breathing in time, or in syncopation, accepting that this is how it is, that things have to happen this way, first one, then the other, each one in turn, devising a unique, singular present, which immediately escapes the three of us, forever.

Now I see them collecting the cards in their big mitts, piling some on top of others into two decks confronting each other from an equal distance on either side of the table, Jaime's with blue arabesques, Boca's orange, and it looks like they've finished their game.

I feel a little lonely. I've no one to talk to about this approaching maternity.

Tomorrow is the thirtieth of October. My due date is in the middle of February, it's all happened so suddenly, and I couldn't do anything about it.

FORTY

We can get married. Jaime is speaking, in the dark, without showing his face. We got back from Luján a short while ago, from a barbecue at Héctor and Marta's to celebrate the twins' eighth birthday. We went to bed straight away, slightly nauseous from so much meat. The sheets were damp, almost wet. In the middle of the night I got up to pee. In the bathroom I looked at myself in the mirror and thought that I didn't look quite as bad as I had in recent months. In the dark, I sensed where the bed was and lay down again on my side, the gate side. It had been that way since the beginning, me on this side, Jaime closer to the other Jaime. Dead or alive. It's so strange to have something in my stomach that's going to be someone. I stroke myself, I feel it with my open palm, I wait a while, nothing. I wonder when it was. That first time, when I didn't even come?

Héctor and Marta treat me as if I'm one of the family now. The twins adore me, they say I'm their favourite aunt.

I'm scared. I close my eyes to try to stop thinking and, right then, Jaime decides to speak. Wasn't he asleep? We can get married, he says and doesn't insist, he's not interested in my answer, that's all he has to say.

I re-read the notes that I've written over the last few months on Cabred, Huret, the colony and the lunatics, and it seems like a distant memory, adolescent and boring. There are about fifty sheets or more, the first few handwritten on both sides, the rest printed from the computer, normal type, double-spaced. I scan the pages, and it's enough to catch a sentence or a few words at random to guess the context, I know what follows. It's nothing more than that, a collection of sentences linked by sufficient common sense. I lost interest, I can't deny it, and yet for almost five months my head was full of loonies: loonies on horseback, bricklayer loonies, uniformed loonies, in blue or orange, or both, blue trousers and orange sweatshirt, loonies with no clothes on, undressing in the middle of something, loonies kneading bread, hand over hand over hand, frenetically, old-style loonies, deranged, less neurotic but more insane, loonies who don't look like loonies, who bite their lips, just slightly, like anyone else, but who only think about that, about biting their lips, loonies who are practically philosophers, who say things that leave us open-mouthed, as if to say: Look what the loony said, lost loonies, loonies who get beaten up, with clean blows, and who one day, without explanation, start to receive fewer blows, or secret blows, out of sight of the other loonies, and more, many more, all of them, dead loonies, like the one that Jaime found amongst the weeds of the nursery, almost albino, his eyes wide open, or the one who appeared hanging from a branch above the clay oven, his feet stained with soot from the smoke that kept churning out, and the loonies who no one looks for, who nobody reclaims, who they call anything, whatever name comes to them, loonies fucking, never coming, all the loonies, in a row, ready to enter the catalogue, invented loonies, who are the vast majority, because it's easy to invent loonies, nobody makes mistakes inventing loonies, anything could be true. They're there, even though they no longer interest me, they tell me a load of things, but it isn't the same. I'm bored.

The dream from the other night returns, it never ends. Still in Rio de Janeiro, it still seems as though I'm going to kill them all. But I don't kill them.

A car with tinted windows stops by the gate. It beeps three times. The first two short, the third sustained. I approach slowly. I don't walk as quickly as before.

One of the front windows opens, on the passenger side, and Eloísa appears. She's dressed entirely in black. A bit like a goth, but not entirely. She raises her hand, waves and shouts my name. She's had her hair cut, it's uneven, two long tufts cover half her face. We say hello without opening the gate. She kisses me on one cheek, then the other, and in passing she brushes my mouth. Only just. Now she extends her arms, to see me better, and she says or protests, with emotion or anger: So it was true. She strokes my belly, without really touching me much, from a distance. And you, I ask. I'm good, and in my ear: I've got a boyfriend. And she gestures for the person sitting in the car listening to music to get out. And he gets out, rather ungainly, his hair tousled, chewing red gum. She introduces us. They look at each other, they smile, I smile. And he says: How's it going? Fine, I say, hi. I don't know whether they want to come in, I don't know whether I want them to stay. Since I'm unsure, we say goodbye. Eloísa winks at me. I hate her.

I want to talk to you, says Jaime and immediately plugs his mouth with a cigarette as if he regrets saying it. But he takes courage and continues: About what I said to you the other times, the other night, you haven't said anything. About what? I ask and play dumb. About getting married, he says. Jaime speaks without looking at me, uncomfortable, and I can't believe what I'm hearing. He pauses. The first thing that comes to me is: There's no need, we're fine like this, we can carry on like this. Jaime doesn't answer, he smokes and becomes sad. Let's see what happens, I say and stretch out a hand that stays in the air, like a silent word that Jaime doesn't catch. He nods, obedient, incapable of arguing. It's the first time a man has proposed to me.

I spend all night crying, in the dark, locked in the bathroom so that Jaime doesn't see me.

FORTY-ONE

It's New Year next week. In the countryside you barely notice. Meanwhile, here, in the city, the year is coming to an end all around. In the faces, in the scents, in the speed of things.

I'm in a bar, sitting by the window. Yasky should be about to arrive. We arranged to meet at half twelve. There are five minutes to go. It had been several months since he called. His voice was different, more serious, hardened. Can we see each other tomorrow? It's important, he said. It's to do with your friend.

I didn't say anything to Jaime. He would have wanted to come with me and I preferred to go alone. Recently, we've barely been apart for a minute. What with his retirement, Jaime has begun to work less. He hardly goes to the hospital any more, he says there's no cure for that nursery. He doesn't know what to do with his time. Neither do I. I never go out. I spend my time in bed, now and then I read something and I watch a lot of television.

I'm going shopping in Luján, I told him. The same lie as usual. Take the truck, he said. And before I left, seeing me off at the gate: Drive carefully.

On the road, I try to think about Aída, but I can't. Every time I bring her to mind, she escapes me. After everything that's happened, it's an old and faded story. And more than anything, it's very complicated. Why am I going?

Yasky gets out of a taxi. He's let his hair grow long and he's fatter. He looks my way, I signal to him, but he doesn't see me. I go out onto the pavement and now he does, we wave. He crosses the street, and as he approaches he can't conceal his surprise. He looks at my stomach. I smile, I'd forgotten too. Our telephone conversation was very brief, and the truth is that it hadn't occurred to me to tell him. For me, it hadn't been a novelty for quite a while. I didn't know, says Yasky, prolonging the last vowel until he runs out of breath. He seems different, both euphoric and drawn, with new dark circles around his eyes. We start walking. He takes my arm. With the sounds of the street, I'm unable to pay him much attention, and anyway, what I hear doesn't surprise me. At a corner, a traffic light brings us to a halt.

'From the photos, it seems very likely that it's her, although we can't confirm it one hundred per cent.'

We cross the street. We pass a square. I recognise this route, we're a block and a half from the morgue and we're heading in that direction. I don't protest, I let myself be led by Yasky, who hasn't let go of my arm. The weather is very humid, sticky. We walk in silence. When we're almost there, Yasky stops short, gives a serious, elaborate pause and, all at once, without releasing his breath, squeezes my arms at the elbows, arches his brows and looks at me straight on. There's something else, he says, something that doesn't make sense. Another pause and he comes out with it: the autopsy says that she died two days ago. It's inconceivable, but there it is, he concludes, and his mouth stays open.

Yasky lets go of my arms and his stubby hands hesitate in the air for a few seconds until they make bold and clutch mine. He's waiting for me to speak, to answer him, to cry or break down. He's waiting for me to embrace him, waiting for something that I don't give him and he moves away sadly.

The equation is obvious but even so it surprises me: Yasky is still in love with me. And once again, he's used Aída to be able to see me. This time, by devising an impossible tale. He turns his back to me, he can't look at me again, he knows I've found him out and so he goes on with the farce.

We enter the morgue. Like the first time, I follow close behind him. We walk to the end of the corridor. Yasky knocks on the office door, fulfilling his role as court clerk to the last. The enormous ginger guy from the first few visits isn't there; an extremely thin man appears in his place. Yasky introduces us, the man glances at me and makes a grimace with his lips that doesn't quite manage to be a smile. Now they take a couple of steps aside and exchange a few words in low voices. Yasky nods, the other man goes ahead and enters the room, gesturing for us to follow.

We stand around the middle trolley. Yasky looks at the floor, avoiding my eyes. The other man is impatient, he grinds his teeth, swallows saliva and without preamble, lifts the plastic sheet covering Aída's body.

On the way out of the morgue, Yasky asks whether I'm all right and whether I wouldn't like to go for a coffee. I nod, still a bit dazed. It makes no sense, I repeat to myself, and the absurdity of the situation makes me chuckle. I hang my head and the irregularity of the floor tiles ends up disconcerting me. It's as though it's all just a trick of Yasky's. But no, he'd never go that far. And, I'd almost forgotten, it was Aída, slightly changed, but it was her. And it was precisely that which perturbed me most: that she'd cut her hair and plucked her eyebrows, that all those months when I thought she was dead she had been somewhere, she'd rented another flat, she'd gone to a hotel, to a friend's, or wandered through the city, perhaps she'd even had a job, it was madness, to think that Aída had been alive all this time, and so close.

We go into a bar, we sit down at a table set for lunch. I have to say something, I have to express my bewilderment somehow, but Yasky beats me to it.

It's a bit like going back to square one, he says. But so far as our involvement goes, it's case closed. They'll have to open a new investigation. I can't bring myself to ask him anything. Not who found her. Or how. Or where. I stay silent, my mouth half open. Yasky talks, to cover the void. Poor girl, he says.

Beba took care of everything, all the procedures, the funeral director, the cremation and arranging a priest to give the urn extreme unction. She travelled from Asunción as soon as she heard the news. I don't know why she didn't come before, why it was me instead of her who had to come and meet those unknown corpses so many times.

In all these months we hadn't been in contact once. The truth is she looked great, her skin younger than ever, and she had dyed her hair a furious red. She arrived in a funeral car, the only one in the cortège. She was accompanied by a man who was much too young to be her husband and yet embraced her with evident tenderness.

It was a quick goodbye, without tears. The circumstances in which everything had happened discouraged any spirit of a wake. The time that had elapsed, the supposed suicide, Aída's clandestine life, the deceit, the confusion, everything that made this story an episode more delirious than traumatic, gave rise to an unusual funeral, not to mention the fact that it had been decided to cremate the body. I don't know who had taken that decision, whether it was Beba or the judge, Yasky, or Aída herself in the will I never saw.

Jaime insisted so much that in the end I let him accompany me. But I asked him to wait for me in a bar opposite the cemetery. During the half hour that the ceremony lasted, Beba didn't say a word to me, she looked at me only once in passing, but I'm not even sure it was intentional. I didn't really understand the reasons behind her indifference. The only thing I would have wanted to ask was who had ended up with Diki, the crippled dog that Aída had left orphaned.

Yasky, on the other hand, was by my side the whole morning. After the initial shock, a paternal instinct seemed to have awoken in him, or something like it, because he didn't stop referring to my stomach and the closeness of the birth.

Beba and her young boyfriend took a taxi. Yasky said goodbye quickly as he had a hearing in fifteen minutes on the other side of the city, demanding that I promise to let him know when I had news.

As I went down the cemetery steps, there was something, difficult to define, a new sensation that slackened my whole body, like a wave, which sank me to the ground without violence. And there, sitting on the bottom step, with the points of my shoes crossing on the pavement, I realised that my skirt was wet. I had left a pool behind me and a yellowish stain opening in the shape of a fan, it surrounded me, like a shadow. I didn't have time to wonder what had happened, people came from all sides to help me, a man in a waterproof, a policeman and a woman holding a child by the hand. All together, all at the same time.

'It's nothing serious,' I heard behind me, 'her waters have broken.'

It was a woman's voice, deliberate and confident.

EPILOGUE

It was Simón's first birthday on Saturday. He's a quiet baby, cute, he barely cries, just the right amount. In the evening, Jaime held a barbecue to celebrate. Eloísa came with her new boyfriend, and Héctor and Marta, the twins, Boca and his nephew Martín. Guido was there for a while but he had to leave early because some friends were playing in a bar in the capital.

A year has passed and everything goes on in much the same way. Everyone fulfils his own destiny. Eloísa left school and is working as a waitress in a pizzeria in Luján. We see less of each other. We hardly see each other at all. Her new boyfriend is local, an ordinary guy with a kind face. You can tell he's in love.

Jaime planted a vegetable garden behind the stable. He sowed courgettes, potatoes, pumpkins, spinach, green leaf lettuce, chicory, garlic and tomatoes. He says the first harvest will be ready next month. I take care of the baby and the

house. It's a different life, I'd never have imagined it, but it's
not bad. Sometimes, when I can't sleep, I find myself switching on the computer and re-reading all that madness about
Open Door, and it's as though someone else wrote it. One day,
who knows, I'll do something with all that.

A few weeks ago I received a postcard from Yasky from
Florianópolis in Brazil: a sunset, half sky, half sea, taken from
the coast. He tells me that he received a research grant in
international law. He's studying Portuguese at the university
and preparing his doctoral thesis. He says that it's changed
his life. It's not hard to see why.

At around midnight, after eating, Jaime and Boca proposed a
trip into the woods to hunt partridges. Little Martín and the
twins gave a shout of joy.

The preparation is the best part: cleaning out the
shotguns, sorting the cartridges, dividing up tasks. Eloísa,
Martín, the twins and I are all going. Marta is staying
behind to take care of Simón, and Héctor doesn't like guns.
Eloísa's boyfriend isn't coming either, because he doesn't
feel like it, or because Eloísa won't let him, it's hard to tell
which.

We wrap ourselves up in anticipation of the dew. Jaime
drives, Boca and the boys are in the back of the pick-up, Eloísa
and I in the front. Eloísa switches on the radio and turns the
dial from end to end until she picks up a Ramones riff. Jaime
complains silently. Eloísa moves as if she's dancing. She keeps
elbowing me in the stomach. Jaime gets tired and turns
down the volume. Eloísa imitates his face for my benefit, the

face of a grumpy old man. They're never going to get along.

We arrive in a clearing. Boca and Jaime lean their hefty shotguns on their shoulders, Martín has to make do with an air rifle. The twins carry the ammunition. Eloísa and I follow everything from the outside, as spectators.

In silence, we penetrate the heart of the wood with the obligatory respect that the night imposes on us, all its stars sparkling in chorus.

It gets late and there's no excitement to keep us awake. I wonder how far we're going to walk. It must be after two, there's not a soul to be heard. Dawn in the countryside is enough to frighten anyone.

Finally we stop. Jaime and Boca scan the dark, even ground with their guns pointing at the earth. Eloísa and I share a split trunk to sit and rest a while. Martín and the twins entertain themselves with the cartridges. I look at the sky and think about Aída. I'll never understand her.

I get the feeling that I can hear those guitar rounds that the gypsies used to play. Quite far off, but unmistakeable. If I tell Eloísa she'll think I'm mad. Better keep it to myself.

Right then, all of a sudden, when it seems that nothing else is going to happen, as if in a bad film, a weird B-movie, a beam of incandescent light at the level of the horizon dazzles us straight on, here and there lighting up the plain. We stop, all at the same time, avoiding each other's eyes. We don't want to believe it, we'd rather it passed by quickly, that it was an optical illusion. But the brightness grows, changes colour, from perfect white to a pale red that intensifies into a fiery red and suddenly extinguishes, then lights up again as it did at the start. It hypnotises us, this soft sphere between the sky and the earth. Martín passes me his rifle and disappears behind a tree. I feel like peeing too. Jaime moves forward ever so slightly, a couple of steps, Boca does the same. They fix their gaze on this inconceivable apparition. They start walking again, straight towards it. In the second row, by mutual agreement, Eloísa, the twins and I follow them, without joking about. Martín reaches us at a sprint and joins the line.

The word UFO quashes all others in my head. It's the strangest thing to happen to me recently. Is it possible? As we approach, it's as if I were relinquishing all my prejudices, as if it were the most natural thing in the world to have an extraterrestrial experience at some stage in life. To make contact with the beyond. Someone, Martín or one of the twins, coughs to attract attention and says: Let's go back. It sounds like a joke but nobody laughs. I can't bring myself to say anything. Boca murmurs something in Jaime's ear. The thing is getting closer, taking on increasingly monstrous yet familiar shapes. It's a kind of rotating house, flat and long, emitting thick rings of light that start to illuminate our path. Like a circus. The tip of the rifle bangs against my knee and only now do I realise that Martín never asked for it back. He's obviously lost interest.

Everything becomes so real and so dangerous. Boca raises his shotgun to his shoulder, pointing at the spaceship, either in jest, to prepare himself, or because he's afraid and this is how he expresses it. I can't see properly but I'm sure that Jaime disapproves.

We advance. Confusion makes way for a certain logic.

Things gradually begin to humanise. We recover our breath. We stop about ten metres away and we can make everything out perfectly: the trucks, the trailers, the cranes, the people toing and froing, the row of spotlights of varying intensities. Eloísa separates herself from the group and disappears into that world which, until a few minutes ago, we thought was from another planet.

Eloísa returns and tells us: It's full of guys dressed like natives, they're filming an advert. Fake natives, says Boca, laughing hard. And to think we believed they were Martians. I was hallucinating that it was a spaceship, says one of the twins. We all were, corrects the other.

Shall we go and see? asks Jaime. Martín and the twins are enthusiastic. We'd better leave the guns here, in case they still think we're the enemy, says Boca. We laugh.

Go, we'll stay here to keep an eye on them, Eloísa convinces them as she interlaces her fingers with mine. So Jaime, Boca and the boys, rather timidly, step into the film set.

Eloísa and I forget the guns and everything that's been left on the ground. We lose ourselves in the night, turning our backs to all the commotion. No one sees us. Eloísa hugs me tightly, I can tell she's horny. We kiss like a couple of teenagers, devouring each other in secret, against the trunk of a giant *ombú* tree. I feel happy.

AFTERWORD

Argentinian critic Alberto Manguel has argued that the third revolution in Hispanic literature hasn't happened yet. He says that after Cervantes' *Don Quixote* and Borges' *Ficciones*, nothing revolutionary has come out of literature written in Spanish. And according to Manguel, the third revolution will not happen until writers face up to Borges' challenge.

What challenge? Borges contended you couldn't approach truth, ultimate meaning or ideal beauty directly because doing so, and being able to experience such things as the face of God, the meaning of the universe, or truth, would turn out to be a nightmare. The experience would be blinding and destructive. This is what happens, for instance, in David Lynch's films: whenever his protagonist encounters in reality what she has been dreaming of or fantasising about, the result is catastrophic. What you should do is approach meaning indirectly, moving around it in circles while embracing the multi-layered surface of the real. Fiction, which structures reality, is like a candle moving about in a tomb: ultimately contingent and yet necessary. That is, if one is to keep one's sanity amid impending darkness.

It is best to proceed by revealing one layer of appearance after another in the same way one peels an onion, but without expecting to get at the hard kernel. Warning: onions do not have hard kernels.

For example, with fantasy horror fiction, Borges counselled against describing or naming the monster. Instead, describe the environment, the alien architecture that would fit the creature, or relate to it only by considering its effects on everything else. Those who go straight for the revelation in such stories end up crazy. This is why Borges thought H. P. Lovecraft's tales were brilliant but ultimately flawed: Lovecraft could not resist the urge to name his monsters.

In contrast, Iosi Havilio proceeds as Borges recommended: he describes effects rather than their causes and works through narrative rather than by naming. In fact, Havilio has gone further than Borges thought possible. In *Open Door*, Havilio suggests there may not be a single, comprehensible cause at all. Even if named it remains hidden, like God in the many Borgesian stories inspired by Jewish mysticism or by Kafka.

There may be an exception to this rule: on the back cover of the Spanish edition, Havilio names his monster: '*capitalismo + sálvese quien pueda*' ('capitalism + every man for himself'). Yet his revelation upholds the rule rather than undermining it. This is not the Tetragrammaton; it isn't the revelatory name of God. Naming the creature here does not make it visible. As Havilio suggests, today's monsters are quite unlike the iconic monsters of Borges' time – the Hitlers, Pinochets and Videlas. Our gods and monsters, our tyrants and profiteers, are faceless.

If this is the case, if Havilio has dared to name his monster without spoiling his story, then he has not only stood up to Borges' challenge. He has won. He's not the only one, but Iosi Havilio stands out among a generation of Latin American writers who represent something new in literature. The third revolution in Hispanic literature has arrived.

Great literature, which like *Open Door* often develops a story of death foretold, does not seek to pacify its audience by producing catharsis after a moment of transgressive sex or violence. Rather, it aims at harnessing such violence, turning it into desire for change and then forming this desire into new law. As we all know, the law, as it is now and has been in the past, is somebody else's desire – the desire of the powerful and the wealthy. Great literature defines itself against such desire. Put bluntly, great literature is revolutionary.

There is a lot of sex and violence in *Open Door*, but it is never gratuitous. The narrative opens with a ritual sacrifice of the kind that can only take place between lovers. When the protagonist arrives for the first time at Open Door and meets Jaime, we are told his role is that of the substitute: *On the way to the stable, Jaime tells me that the horse is called Jaime, like him.* One replaces the other. Likewise Jaime, the empty vessel, will replace a lost lover. A few paragraphs earlier, our protagonist met a girl staring at her from the window of a run-down village store. She is also a substitute. Like the characters, all moments – present, past, future – are identical and exchangeable. There's no true novelty, only the repetition of the same. Something, somebody, has made time and people equivalent and interchangeable.

Sacrifice is a game of substitutions. In ancient times, this was the principle of magic. If you knew somebody's name, you could control, seduce, even kill that person. That sacrificial game hovers over every erotic encounter in the novel. Are these passionate encounters or are the lovers mindlessly exchanging one another? Havilio's descriptions of love-making are masterful precisely because they never let us decide. Is love possible in the era of *capitalismo + sálvese quien pueda*?

Nothing here is quite what it seems. The snow melts and the ice cracks beneath your feet. There is a story within the story: that of Open Door, the psychiatric hospital that gives its name to both town and novel.

Our protagonist discovers an account of Open Door among the books in Jaime's house. She's no Borges, but soon enough she is on her way to the library. The librarian confirms that it is a rare find and begins translating it. Jaime denies the book is his. There seems to be a tantalising secret hidden in its pages.

What if all the incidents I've touched on are merely the fantasies of a patient interned in Open Door? After all, this is Argentina, where psychoanalysis is king and a session with one's analyst is as common as a session with one's beauty therapist in Brazil or Colombia. The aim is not too dissimilar: plastic surgery for the soul. The librarian's translation reveals the pioneering therapeutic technique that gave Open Door its name and prestige. What if we're all mad, oblivious to the fact that the whole world of capitalism + every man for himself is one big Open Door? Isn't capitalism, in fact, a kind of plastic surgery for the soul?

Re-read this book, because nothing in this novel *is* quite what it seems. Not because there is some ultimate kernel of meaning waiting behind the lines of the last chapter, but because there are only appearances. The story remains in the surface, like smooth snow to the skier, who glides expertly over it oblivious to the fact he is heading towards a precipice. You have in your hands a masterpiece.

Oscar Guardiola-Rivera
London, June 2011

Dear readers,

We rely on subscriptions from people like you to tell these other stories – the types of stories most UK publishers would consider too risky to take on.

Our subscribers don't just make the books physically happen. They also help us approach booksellers, because we can demonstrate that our books already have readers and fans. And they give us the security to publish in line with our values, which are collaborative, imaginative and 'shamelessly literary' (the *Guardian*).

All of our subscribers:

- receive a first edition copy of every new book we publish
- are thanked by name in the books
- are warmly invited to contribute to our plans and choice of future books

BECOME A SUBSCRIBER, OR GIVE A SUBSCRIPTION TO A FRIEND

Visit andotherstories.org/subscribe to become part of an alternative approach to publishing.

Subscriptions are:

£20 for two books per year

£35 for four books per year

£50 for six books per year

The subscription includes postage to Europe, the US and Canada. If you're based anywhere else, we'll charge for postage separately.

OTHER WAYS TO GET INVOLVED

If you'd like to know about upcoming events and reading groups (our foreign-language reading groups help us choose books to publish, for example) you can:

- join the mailing list at: andotherstories.org/join-us
- follow us on twitter: @andothertweets
- join us on Facebook: And Other Stories

This book was made possible by everyone who subscribed to *Open Door* before its first English-language publication in the UK. Thank you!

Our Subscribers

Aca Szabo
Alexandra Cox
Ali Smith
Alisa Holland
Alison Hughes
Amanda Jones
Amanda Hopkinson
Ana Amália Alves da Silva
Ana María Correa
Anca Fronescu
Andrea Reinacher
Andrew Tobler
Andrew Blackman
Angela Kershaw
Anna Milsom
Anne Christie
Anne Withers
Anne Jackson
Barbara Glen
Bárbara Freitas
Briallen Hopper
Bruce Millar
Carlos Tamm
Carol O'Sullivan
Caroline Rigby
Catherine Mansfield
Cecilia Rossi
Charles Boyle
Charlotte Ryland
Christina MacSweeney
Claire Williams
Clare Horackova
Daniel Hahn
Daniel Gallimore
David Wardrop
Debbie Pinfold
Denis Stillewagt
Elena Cordan

Emma Staniland
Eric Dickens
Eva Tobler-Zumstein
Fiona Quinn
Fiona Miles
Gary Debus
Genevra Richardson
Georgia Panteli
Geraldine Brodie
Hannes Heise
Helen Leichauer
Helen Weir
Henriette Heise
Henrike Lähnemann
Iain Robinson
Ian Goldsack
Jennifer Higgins
Jimmy Lo
Jo Luloff
John Clulow
Jonathan Ruppin
Jonathan Evans
Joy Tobler
Judy Garton-Sprenger
Julia Sanches
Juro Janik
K L Ee
Kate Griffin
Kate Pullinger
Kate Wild
Kevin Brockmeier
Krystalli Glyniadakis
Laura Watkinson
Laura McGloughlin
Liz Tunnicliffe
Lorna Bleach
Louise Rogers
Maisie Fitzpatrick

Margaret Jull Costa
Marion Cole
Nichola Smalley
Nick Stevens
Nick Sidwell
Nicola Hearn
Nicola Harper
Olivia Heal
Peter Law
Peter Blackstock
Philip Leichauer
Polly McLean
Rachel McNicholl
Rebecca Whiteley
Rebecca Miles
Rebecca Carter
Rebecca K. Morrison
Réjane Collard
Ros Schwartz
Ruth Martin
Samantha Schnee
Samantha Christie
Samuel Willcocks
Sophie Moreau Langlais
Sophie Leighton
Sorcha McDonagh
Steph Morris
Susana Medina
Tamsin Ballard
Tania Hershman
Tim Warren
Tomoko Yokoshima
Verena Weigert
Vivien Kogut Lessa de Sa
Will Buck
Xose de Toro

Current & Upcoming Books by And Other Stories

Title: *Open Door*
Author: Iosi Havilio
Translator: Beth Fowler
Editor: Bethan Ellis
Proofreader: Ellie Robins
Typesetter: Charles Boyle
Series and Cover Design: Joseph Harries
Format: B Format with French flaps
Paper: 55# Heritage Book Cream, 400 PPI
Printer: Edwards Brothers Malloy,
Ann Arbor, Michigan, USA